Instruments of Sun, Ice & Sand:

KOZINIAC DYNASTY

VOLUME ONE

SADIQUE O. GRANT

COPYRIGHT

ISBN 978-1-3999-9104-9

Published by Sadique O. Grant

Printed in the United Kingdom

DEDICATION

In an effort to not forget anyone, I would like to give a collective thanks. To those who encouraged me to keep writing, to those who gave up their time to read and listen to my ideas, and to those who inspired me to continue even in the face of self-doubt.

May this story capture your imagination as it did mine.

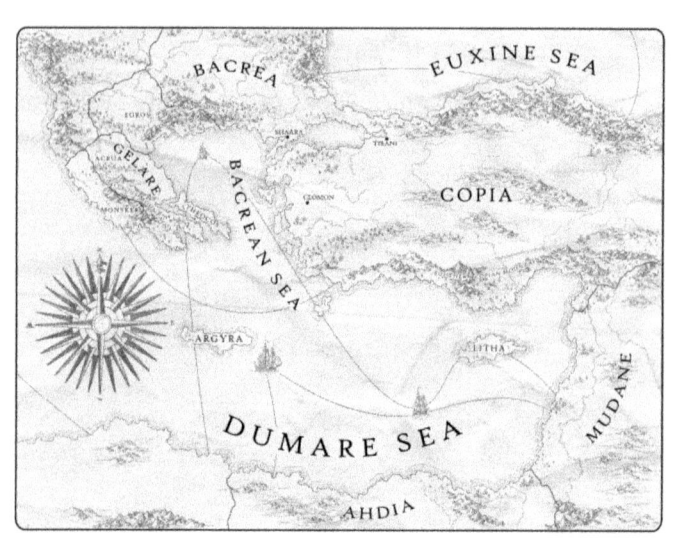

'Before The House... Was The Foundation'

SHAARA

285 BM

1

The ocean is never still. Tonare gazed out from the front of the bireme, eyeing the bit of shore he could make out. As the ship's massive hull rocked beneath him, he swayed in perfect unison with it. The sky was grey fluff. The sea was a leaden hue. Just over his shoulder stood Posidius, his face a stark contrast to Tonare's with its expression of quiet concern. They now entered the Bacrean Sea, slowly approaching the two island forts responsible for the coastal protection of the king's capital. Flanked on both sides, the rocky islets dwarfed the bireme and Tonare could feel the galley being scrutinised from a vantage point. However, he was confident this scrutiny would not last long. The blue sails and the face of the bull upon it would quell any anxiety and suspicion.

They continued to approach the shoreline. Beacons remained unlit, which helped to reinstall some composure to Posidius.

"My liege," Posidius started. "It would have been prudent to send word first."

Tonare looked over his shoulder and presented a wry smile. The bireme was now approaching the stony jetty, a structure almost forming a semi-circle, if not for the gap in the middle. It was through this gap that they entered the harbour. Gently, the cacophony of sounds revealed itself. The soft crashing of waves, the yells of sailors and the general busyness created a symphony that could cause one's head to throb, but Tonare found serenity in the din.

2

Shaara was a city on the coast of the Bacrean Sea. It was alive. The city drew merchants and traders from across the Dumare, giving birth to a hub of commerce and culture. Tonare's galley had docked, and he stood waiting. First, for Posidius to finish instructing the sailors and second, for senior army personnel to greet him. He felt some eyes from the crowd as he waited; no doubt the blue sails stood out. It wasn't just that though. The white chlamys that hugged his shoulders and the solid gold fibula that held it there gave some indication as to his socio-economic class. He had a freshness to him, even on a day that the grey skies seemed to have sapped the colour out of everything... He appeared bright.

Tonare could now see a small military unit approaching. Everyone wore armour except for the man leading them. Posidius now emerged at the prince's side, ready to give a formal introduction. As the man proceeded towards them, Posidius began.

"Prince Tonare of Ahdia, first-born son of Kozin I Salvator. Rightful heir." There was much pride in the voice.

The man gave a small bow before he said, "Mekon, navarch of Shaara. I greet you with grace in the name of our king." He then continued almost reluctantly, "Forgive me, prince... but I received no word of your arrival."

"The matter is delicate," Tonare said drily.

"The sails of your ship ceased my hand from giving command. A command that would have seen you at the bottom of the sea, next to Thaton himself." There was a pause for a moment.

"I'm blessed to have the protection of Otia," Tonare replied with a smile.

The navarch took a moment before he spoke, seemingly fishing. "I wish not to offend. I have not had the honour of meeting any of King Kozin's sons, and if we were to be giving audience... the army would have prior knowledge."

During this exchange, Posidius noticed that Mekon's left hand remained glued to his red scabbard.

Mekon went further, "Why am I to believe you are a prince of Ahdia?" He was beginning to cast a light on his distrustfulness.

"*Cur non creditis*?" Tonare replied sharply. There was some surprise existing in Mekon's eyes. Posidius, already close to the prince, intended to invade his space even more. An attempt to whisper nervous words. This ceased when Tonare raised his right hand with a clenched fist. He already knew Posidius' mind. Tonare's left hand was concealed by his white woollen cloak this entire time and now it was to peek.

When his left arm revealed itself, it was a splendour. Tonare held a sceptre; it was of pure solid gold. The orb at the very top sparkled with encrusted emeralds and rubies. The filigree work below the orb was a latticework pattern, made from fine strands of gold. Mekon was close enough to gaze upon it and the sight dazzled him. Scenes of Kozin's victories and his crowning as Ahdian king were engraved on the shaft. Its authenticity was indisputable.

Mekon offered a gentle bow before he spoke, "We are honoured... Excelletem."

3

Tonare was now on horseback and inside the city walls. Posidius rode next to him with Mekon ahead, guiding them to the palace. Directly behind them was a small group of military men on horses. This kind of entourage naturally drew attention. Making their way through the winding streets, the prince offered a smile to those who were watching him. Carts rumbled over cobblestone; blacksmiths hammers clanged at metalwork and merchants babbled away in a fervent attempt to sell their wares.

As the prince looked to his right, he could see Posidius wrinkling his nose every so often. A reaction to the pungent smell of animal. The earlier briny smell of the coast was preferable. As they entered deeper into the city, the smell of spices dominated.

Tonare continued to observe the everyday people; they're the ones that are the heart of a city. Providing the necessary labour to house, feed and clothe, utilise strategic resources to aid military might. Of course, the utilisation of luxury resources to boost coin and allow the blue bloods to wear the finest robes, the finest jewellery and drink the finest wine. *Land and labour,* Tonare thought, *from governor to king.* His mind carried him back to a story he was told, roughly around the age of eleven. A story he felt that was intended to teach him necessity. It was about the current King Sharadin, back when he was just a governor, free from the fatigue and the patches of yellow on his skin that now marked his days. As governor, he founded a city in his name and had visions of a prosperous city. Culturally rich with pleasing architecture. But who was to make it such? Nearby cities, well-established for years, offered little reason for people to migrate to this new city.

What quality of life awaited them? Sharadin, determined to see his vision realised, removed the choice. He methodically orchestrated the destruction of neighbouring cities, not merely removing choice but ensuring that his new metropolis thrived on the forced influx of its new residents. A necessary action for his vision to come true.

Yes, father, I understand necessity, Tonare thought. What is a first-born son that never fulfils accession? *This city is ripe*. Envy trickled into the prince's heart.

Large blocks of stone composed the two watchtowers. A surface full of crevices and fissures, rough and uneven. Subdued in colour, a natural grey. A striking contrast to what Tonare's eyes would soon see next. The military personnel posted there acknowledged Mekon, and they entered through an opening in the tower walls.

They were at the feet of the propylaeum; it rose before them, its magnificence towering above with each step they took up the wide staircase. The sound of horseshoe clopping echoed loudly, amplified by the sheer scale of the structure. The propylaeum was constructed with pentelic marble, something the visitors from Ahdia could have appreciated more, its surface gleaming under a generous sun, revealing subtle veins. Today, however, the marble appeared muted, its grandeur conquered by the overcast sky, casting a solemn tone over its majestic form.

The monumental gateway had a colonnade façade, marble so smooth one could feel it through their eyes. With conceit, the large construction imposed itself upon them. Nearing the end of the staircase, the visitors beheld the ornamentation. The tympanum relief depicted the patroness of the city – Byra goddess of the harvest. As assimilation grew, people considered her as one and the same as Otia.

Her head held high, Byra's regal posture and the symbols she held – a sheaf of wheat in her left hand raised above her head and a cornucopia in her right – were not just mere decorations. They were profound emblems of prosperity and abundance, deeply revered by the citizens.

For a few moments the ceiling of the propylaeum covered their heads, the sound of hooves striking marble resonated with a clarity, as if the very stones were singing. As they emerged on the other side, entering the royal district, Tonare could feel a struggling breeze against his face. The air warm and heavy. In the distance, the royal palace stood, to one side of it, a temple. Probably the largest temple of the city, it was dedicated to Byra-Otia. The smell of burning incense escaped from it, not completely masking the smell of rotting animal – which represented a good portion of the votive offerings.

As they drew closer to the palace, the greenery of its gardens appeared as a vibrant spectacle against the grey day, fighting to inject colour into the dull atmosphere. Tonare could feel a sense of nervousness taking small bites at his gut. His exterior though, remained regal. His subconscious mind telling. He thought he had good grounds to request the king's support. As a man of principle and tradition, he should oblige him. Prince Tonare was now staring, but of course not really capturing the images. The noise of their horses provided the rhythm to aid his trance-like state.

4

The front yard had an aura of timeless elegance and natural beauty. Lush greenery and vibrant blooms harmoniously adorned the landscape, creating a picturesque scene. The periphery of the garden featured meticulously manicured hedges. This gave off a vibe of enclosure and added structure to the design. They had dismounted and walked the path that led to the front of the palace. Tonare was staring earnestly at the palace entrance, waiting for the king to emerge from in between the colonnades. Posidius, who is usually attentive, was not paying attention to the anticipation of the king's presence. He allowed himself to be distracted by the centrepiece of the circular plaza. A grand fountain portraying the features of the king, standing majestically. It made him seem almost God like.

"Your attention, Posidius," Tonare whispered instruction.

"Apologies, Excelletem," Posidius replied.

He turned his back on the fountain and faced the palace. Unable to subdue his cautious nature, he requested to speak. Tonare nodded in reluctance.

"My liege, I think it best if you make the purpose of our visit known upon greeting," Posidius advised, as he leaned closer, his voice lost in the yard's clatter. Tonare looked at him from the corner of his eyes. The advisor continued in a whisper, "If you do not, my liege, the king and his counsel will assume the reason they most desire." Posidius was really whispering now, "Then the disappointment will make it difficult for your request to find the king's favour. Also, we must consider the king's condition. It is likely to make him more cautious, and with Superare's ambitions in Copia looming—"

"I am aware of Ellisar's rumoured ambitions," Tonare interrupted. "And while the king's health wanes, it does not dull his mind."

The prince's agitation was now growing, the root cause remained undiscovered. It would have been easy to blame Posidius, but the wait for the king was equally taxing. Tonare knew Posidius spoke no false words. The rumoured intentions of Superare were spreading, like wildfire leaping from treetop to treetop. Certain messages would be more favourable, and his presence here could lead to those conclusions. The king's retinue then informed them that the king reconsidered meeting them at the entrance of the palace.

So, they escorted Tonare and Posidius through corridors. Amidst the resplendent halls of the grand palace, the marble floors echoed with measured steps. The air carried the scent of laurel and myrtle, while the intricate frescoes on the palace wall demanded a gaze or two. As they approached the Throne Room, military men swung open the towering doors, revealing the heart of the palace. Tonare tightened the grip on his sceptre. In the middle of the room, King Sharadin sat upon a colossal ruby-embedded throne, the centrepiece, radiating regality and reflecting the king's love of the gemstone. To the left of the throne stood Paterocles, the king's eldest son. Fascinating the stark contrast in stature between them. Paterocles had a frame that suggested nimbleness; he was slender. However, the king had a build that suggested he was capable of swinging an axe. A man of average height with a protruding gut. A member of the king's retinue gave an official introduction, although he couldn't state the purpose of Tonare's visit. They began to walk toward the throne, carved marble columns adorned with intricate grapevine motifs, framed a vast space. Tonare could feel a heaviness attempting to interfere with his legs. King Sharadin, draped in a toga of deep crimson, rose from his ruby-encrusted throne as Prince Tonare and Posidius approached. A welcoming gleam danced in his eyes, for he expected this meeting to forge an alliance, a prospect that invigorated him. With a regal flourish, King Sharadin extended his hand toward the approaching visitors. His hand trembled slightly, a quiver that he masked with a swift movement. "Welcome, Prince Tonare and his counsel Posidius," boomed King Sharadin with a robust voice that resonated across the Throne Room. "May the grace of Byra guide your steps." Beside him, Paterocles nodded in acknowledgement, his features a mix of curiosity and measured composure. "It warms my heart to host you within these walls," continued Sharadin, his enthusiasm palpable. "Bring wine!" he commanded a servant girl, then paused, momentarily losing his train of thought before recollecting with a slight clearing of his throat. "We have the finest wine of all lands," King Sharadin proclaimed with a boast that seemed as much for his own court's ears as for his guests.

Tonare wasn't in the mood for much wine, but to refuse the gesture... Just as he was thinking amid the king's excitement, he met Posidius' gaze briefly. A subtle reminder of an earlier warning. "Autokrator," began Tonare, his voice carefully modulated to mask his reluctance, "I am deeply honoured by your welcome."

"The honour is mine," the king replied with much enthusiasm. The robustness of his voice travelled across the room. "Tell me Tonare... how many women do you take? I shall have your bed filled this night." Tonare had a bashful expression on his face and couldn't find a reply. King Sharadin continued, "Perhaps you have the ways of your father, too consumed in thoughts beyond mortal men to be concerned with desires of the flesh. Or you are a man of similar kind to myself, *reasonable desires.* Or could it be that you have a grand appetite, that of Tyvius, bless the Orange Cunt."

Tonare forced a congenial smile, attempting to mask his truest emotions. His eyes couldn't help but draw towards the throne, a magnificent creation of gold and rubies that seemed to pulsate with an inner fire. Beside the throne stood a piece of furniture crafted from the rugged remnants of a colossal tree. The tree stump possessed an undeniable rustic charm. The heartwood clenched a red double-headed axe. He met Posidius' gaze again, a gnawing reminder. "Autokrator," Tonare continued, his voice carrying a subtle tremor of unease, "Might I request a private audience? The matter I wish to discuss necessitates discretion."

The king's jovial expression flickered, replaced by a mild suspicion that danced across his eyes like a fleeting shadow. Paterocles stood nearby, observing the unfolding dynamics keenly. "A private audience?" Sharadin questioned, his voice laced with intrigue and a hint of caution. "Very well, let us adjourn to the Council Chamber."

The Council Chamber was a more intimate setting, still regal but devoid of the awe-inspiring presence of the grand throne. A bastion of political intrigue and strategic thought. A long, polished table stretched down the centre, it boasted a deep hue resembling aged wine. Its surface, smooth to the touch, displayed intricate wood grain patterns akin to the gentle ripples of a tranquil sea. The king's imposing chair was at the head of the table. Sharadin steadily carried himself through the elongated room toward it, trailing a finger on the table's surface as he went. On his way, he offered some words to Tonare about the recklessness which he displayed by not sending word before arrival.

"I meant no offence to your realm Autokrator. It was an action I felt necessary to conceal my travels," Tonare said. King Sharadin, his crimson toga flowing lavishly, eased into the ornate chair at the table's head. Lines etched into his brow like rivulets on aged parchment, furrows deepened.

"Conceal?" Sharadin muttered, surprised.

"Forgive me Autokrator," Tonare gathered himself. "I know this will cause some dismay, but I am not here on my father's orders." Tonare was at the other end of the elongated room and now slowly started making his way toward the table. The king gestured at a chair and the prince sat, placing his sceptre on the table. A petite servant girl, her presence like a gentle breeze, entered the chamber. Clad in a simple faded linen chiton, her shy eyes cast downward not merely in deference but reflecting the vast gulf between her humble station and the imperial opulence surrounding her, she approached with a jug of wine. She poured with hands that trembled slightly and quickly excused herself.

"Prince Tonare," King Sharadin's voice sounded like thunder, "What is the purpose of your visit here, if not led by your father's will?" The king's features shifted between disappointment and acceptance; Posidius' words rung in Tonare's mind.

"My father has fought many wars; you have been on the same side. Like you, he is one of E'del's Successors."

"He was his most favoured," Sharadin interjected.

"Yes... but he will fail, like so many men before him. In the matter of defeating time."

"Yes... we all will succumb to time. It is a cruel gift, I am told," Sharadin mused, his voice infused with a wistful acceptance of mortality.

"Well, when he receives that gift, he will leave his legacy to Kozin the younger," Tonare spoke while staring into his cup of wine.

"He has uttered these words," Sharadin said, surprised.

"It is clear... he has shown a fondness for the boy," Tonare confessed, a bitter resignation underscored his fraught position in the royal succession.

"Your brother, you mean?" Sharadin said, insinuating that a wrong choice of word was used.

"That boy... stands in the way of my birthright," an icy response left Tonare without a flinch.

King Sharadin, his eyes fixed on Tonare, lifted the goblet to his lips. His weathered hands, bearing gold and onyx rings, gently cradled the vessel. The nails on his fingers were noticeably pale, with a distinct white rim at the tips. The question on his mind was evident in his eyes before the words left his lips. "What are you asking of me? I see you carry the sceptre. Are you sure you are not just a boy, as we all were, feeling removed from your father's love."

"I assure you that is not true," Tonare spoke, swallowing what he perceived to be an insult. "I ask that you support me, as true heir. Based on Egrosian tradition, you are a man he will respect." Tonare's entreat hung in the air like the lingering aroma of wine. Sharadin's gaze turned thoughtful as he looked toward Tonare. He leaned forward, resting his elbows on the table, and spoke with a measured tone, laden with respect for tradition but tinged with concern.

"Prince Tonare, I hold in high regard the ancient customs and rituals of Egros. The concept of succession through the eldest son, shaped by centuries of tradition, is noble and rooted in the very fabric of our lands. Yet, I am mindful of interfering in the domestic affairs of another realm, even one as close to our own as Ahdia."

Tonare nodded, acknowledging the delicate balance. He took a sip of wine; the gesture reflecting his contemplation. "Yes, Autokrator, and I appreciate your understanding," Tonare replied. "However, I come seeking not only your support but a lasting alliance. With me on the throne of Ahdia, you will have a king in your debt. Of course, my father has a few more years left in him, but it will take some time for Ellisar to strategise and gather his army to push west of Copia... If the rumours are true."

Sharadin listened attentively, the mention of Ellisar's ambitions prompting him to contemplate the broader geopolitical implications. He took another sip of wine. The rich vintage filled his mouth, its pronounced tannins releasing a bold and complex flavour. The cup, a vessel of both wisdom and strategy. "I see," Sharadin spoke with a voice that carried much contemplation, "But we cannot be sure of the speed at which Ellisar will act. I know the man. He has probably been coveting land from the moment of E'del's death, or from the day of the egregious orders given by Tyvius, bless the Orange Cunt."

King Sharadin exhaled heavily and drank more wine, the bold notes of the beverage sharpening his focus. "If he has always planned to dominate Copia, then he will travel west faster than you anticipate. And it is your father that will hold the keys to alliance and not you. However, I respect your boldness in coming here, therefore I will discuss the matter with my council. To be clear, Prince Tonare, my first path will be to seek an alliance with your father. If that is not a success, I will look to your terms... It will take some time to determine alliance. I am happy to host you in my realm for that time." Tonare nodded in agreement. Before concluding their discussion, Sharadin's curiosity sparked a change in direction. He leaned back in his throne, eyeing Tonare intently, and broached a topic of philosophical significance. "Tell me, Prince Tonare, what are your thoughts on 'The Loom'? The people of Ahdia believe in its influence, attributing their wisdom and advancement to the universal fabric. Do you not see merit in such beliefs?"

Tonare's expression remained measured, revealing no overt reverence for the concept. He swirled the wine in his goblet, buying time as he gathered his thoughts. "The Loom and its supposed connection to the burnt face ones, is indeed a belief deeply rooted in their culture. However, I am sceptical. Our people, especially those with Kinasci blood, have displayed immense wisdom and capabilities in various fields with no supposed connection to the Loom."

King Sharadin, although respectful of Tonare's perspective, disagreed, leaning forward once more. "Yes, our people possess remarkable skills and intellect, mostly used for conquest and survival," Sharadin confessed. "But there are questions about the greater aspects of our existence. The Loom, as we Egrosians have named it, is not just a tale of connection or prophecy. It represents a deeper, almost mystical understanding of the universe, one that I have observed from afar. Your father, Kozin, seems captivated by this understanding, seeing it as essential for a ruler to grasp these profound undercurrents. Perhaps his hesitance regarding your succession stems from a desire for an heir who mirrors this idea, which he values so dearly."

5

Tonare stood at the window of his chamber, gazing pensively at the expanse of the Bacrean Sea. The cerulean waters stretched as far as his eyes could see, their rhythmic waves murmuring tales of distant lands. His mind wandered, consumed by the weight of his ambitions. The sea breeze wafted through the room, a subtle hint of salt hung in the air, a reminder of the vastness beyond the city walls. The room itself was a haven of opulence, adorned with marble pillars and intricate mosaics that depicted scenes from heroic myths of old. A golden chalice sat on a polished oak table, catching the now emerging sunlight that streamed through the parting clouds, filtering through silk curtains and casting a play of light and shadows across the floor – mirroring the turmoil within Tonare's thoughts.

Unbeknownst to Tonare, Posidius inched stealthily into the room, his steps cushioned by a lavish carpet that depicted swirling aquatic patterns. Tonare's thoughts remained fixed on the horizon; he pondered the legacy he would uphold and the choices that would shape his fate.

After some time, Tonare felt the presence of someone else. He found it strange that Posidius didn't make his presence known, but Posidius explained that the thoughtfulness etched on his face should go undisturbed.

Still looking out the window, Tonare asked, "Do you know why we are here?"

"I would say the desire is the same, but the form and approach have taken on a new shape."

He seems to know my mind, Tonare thought.

Posidius continued, "While the king granted you private audience, I spoke with a few courtiers. The kind prone to idle gossip. There seem to be some rumblings around the matter of succession, Esevia has certain ambitions even though she did not bore King Sharadin's thunder."

"That will not stop her desire," Tonare said thoughtfully. "The king continues to defy orders from the medicus, still indulging in wine. Esevia knows the time to secure her son's place is dwindling."

Posidius concurred without words. Just a slight *hmmm* escaped from him. He waited for Tonare to continue; a white himation draped over his shoulders, contrasting with the toga beneath. His demeanour radiating an air of loyalty and readiness to serve. Tonare fixed his blue icy eyes upon the world beyond the window, while his youthful countenance, framed by dark blonde locks, hinted at the darkness inherited from his mother. The shifting light caught his features as the sun broke through the clouds. The prince was about to speak, but stopped.

"If you are looking for an opportunity," Posidius spoke, feeling that he knew the prince's heart. Tonare turned around and took a glance at Posidius. Yes, Posidius had a picture of their purpose and would follow him into hell if need be.

"Do you know the meaning of Tonare?"

"In the New Tongue?" Posidius asked.

"Yes."

"Thunder..." Posidius answered.

"Yes, I am my father's thunder and yet he will not pass me the crown." Tonare continued to observe the clouds gradually parting, the sun's beams piercing through.

"May I speak with a straight and sharp tongue, my liege," Posidius requested. The prince gave a gesture of consent. *"Sciebas hoc solum iter fore."*

(You knew this would be the only path). The prince was surprised by that remark; he didn't turn around and present his face, but somehow Posidius caught onto his surprise. Maybe his body language conveyed it, a slight flinch perhaps. A few moments passed before Posidius continued, "Sharadin, Autokrator... is married to your half-sister, Esevia. More truly Esevia II. Normally, this would be enough to tie two realms. But your father is different, as you know." Posidius suspended words, waiting to see if the prince would turn around. But he didn't. Posidius went on, "Sharadin, Auto–"

"Cease speaking of him so formally," Tonare interrupted.

"As you wish, Excelletem. Uh... Sharadin is aware of this union not being enough. They have a history and have fought together before, but Sharadin still needs to win his favour."

"You speak of things of which I am aware," Tonare said with an air of frustration.

"In essence my liege, asking him to support you and bring up the matter of Egrosian tradition, puts his desires under threat," Posidius was a little hesitant to go further. "But you knew this."

"Is that so..."

"Yes. Gaining favour on the grounds of Egrosian tradition was the most desirable outcome... It would spare your con–"

"You speak as if you know my mind," Tonare said. His hair was reminiscent of sun-kissed wheat fields caught in the embrace of a gentle breeze.

"Forgive me my liege, but I do," Posidius spoke firm. The prince was about to form words, but this time it was Posidius who interrupted. "You must do the very thing you knew was most possible. Kozin Salvator will look past you, Sharadin will not threaten alliance for your sake. If you want a kingdom.... you must take it." Posidius' words settled like a heavy shroud. An eerie pause. In that pregnant silence, Tonare wrestled with his emotions and the inevitable choice that loomed before him.

"Shrewd you are Posidius," the silence broken, Tonare turned around. "I thought I had kept you in the dark..." The prince's gaze met Posidius' own. "But you knew the dark corners of my mind," Tonare admitted. "With the king's days growing short... Esevia, yearning for her own lineage to succeed. There might be an opportunity for me to use these circumstances."

THE
GREAT
PRETENDER

284 BM

1

The day of Byronia had come alive. Golden hues from the sun coloured the capital city. The festival began to unfold. Anticipation filled the air, as the scent of jasmine and ripe peaches mixed with the fresh grassy aroma, creating a fragrant ambiance in the bustling agora. The city's denizens prepared for the grandeur of the celebrations; a cherished event synonymous with hopes for a prosperous harvest. The procession through the agora marked the commencement of the festivities; weaving its way through stalls covered in vivid silks and festoons of wildflowers.

The royal family, led by King Sharadin and his queen, Esevia II, graced the festival with their presence. Their children – Folas, Sharadin the younger, and Folger accompanied them. With them were the children from his first marriage – Imari, Esevia I and Paterocles. A sea of smiling faces greeted them, the joyous citizenry eager to glimpse their monarch. The crowd focused much of their affection on Paterocles. He stood tall and slender, draped in a soft, ethereal garment of seafoam green – the hue reminiscent of fresh olive leaves kissed by dawn's light. The onlookers admired his poised demeanour and keen eyes, captivated by the prospect of his ascent to power. As cheers rose from the gathering, Paterocles responded with a warm, inclusive smile, his hands occasionally reaching out to touch the fingers extended towards him. His attitude was sharply different from the more reserved acknowledgements of the rest of the royal family. Queen Esevia, watching from a slight distance, maintained a composed smile, but her eyes occasionally narrowed.

The streets of the agora swirled with brilliant colours; music and merriment filled the air. The priesthood led the procession, with the monarchs behind them. Priests and priestesses carried laurel wreaths; some bore ceremonial staffs decorated with vines and ivy. Others carried baskets of fruit and grain, embodying the harvest to come. Tonare and Posidius were present, walking behind the royal family as esteemed guests of the realm. The crowd cheered as the procession moved. Tonare engaged in a thoughtful conversation with Posidius, taking in the colourful celebration.

"How fascinating it is to witness the widespread reverence for Otia," Tonare mused, leaning toward Posidius as the cacophony of the procession swirled around them. His voice dropped to a more confidential tone.

"Indeed, my liege. Otia's influence has transcended distant lands, each embracing her in their own way," Posidius commented quietly. "Her essence remains constant, but the lens through which people perceive and honour her varies."

"Ahh yes..." Tonare said while he gazed at the priesthood, their white robes flowy and seeming to gleam in the daylight. "I am not sure there will be a day when I am fond of the name Byra."

Posidius smiled before he returned words, "I am sure the burnt face ones feel a similar way. Viewing the name 'Otia' as Egrosian tampering. Many still call her Oshu." As the festivities continued, they walked together, contemplating the interconnectedness of cultures and beliefs. The celebration of Otia – Byra – Oshu. Another topic weighted on Posidius' mind, one he felt deserved conversation. He glanced at Tonare with features marked by reluctance. "My liege," Posidius began, choosing words with care. "It has been one year since our arrival... I must ask why you have not yet approached Queen Esevia with your plan."

"Timing Posidius. I needed to understand the court. I also need the queen free from prying eyes and ears," Tonare whispered, barely audible over the festive music and cheers. "We must tread carefully," he added, his words blending with the sound of a nearby lyre player, their conversation concealed under the cloak of celebration.

Posidius understood the intricacies of the situation. The gravity of their intentions, the need for veils and shadows. "Yes, I suppose the courtiers can be intrusive. However, my liege, considering the king's condition, time is a factor. Do you still intend to use Esevia's desire for her son's succession?" Posidius asked. Tonare took a glance at his advisor before reviewing the question. The procession continued, the agora bustling with festivities and fervour, providing a poignant backdrop to their clandestine discussion.

"Indeed, I do," Tonare replied. "A mother's love and aspirations for her own bloodline can be a formidable force. She will of course need Paterocles' position to be sabotaged, with his son's being too young, succession would naturally fall to Folger."

Posidius leaned closer, his voice lowered to a whisper, "That is true, Excelletem. But will she trust you to lend aid?"

Tonare's expression remained stoic. Now and then he cast a smile at the onlookers. "Her desires are something we can manipulate. But we must proceed with caution," Tonare emphasised. A ripple of uncertainty threading through his voice. "One misstep could unravel the very fabric of our designs."

"Understood Excelletem," Posidius affirmed. "May I ask, is it your prestigious Egrosian heritage that makes you so confident that the realm will look to you, in light of Folger's slow wit?"

"Absolutely..." Tonare said before he paused, forcing a smile at one commoner that looked on with awe. "Also, the scribes have informed me that a letter from my father has arrived. I am certain of its contents. Be sure to craft a reply, making it clear. I will not watch his favoured son take what is mine."

2

As the sun descended towards the horizon, the festivities culminated in the amphitheatre. The royal family occupied a distinguished section. King Sharadin wore a deep green toga. Beside him sat Queen Esevia, her peplos a lighter shade of green, cascaded like a gentle stream, contrasting elegantly with the king's attire. Esevia's fair-haired mane shimmered in the fading sunlight, her delicate skin a canvas of pale complexion.

King Sharadin rose, his commanding presence silencing the crowd. The amphitheatre, with its tiered seating and awe-inspiring architecture, had a way of amplifying the grandeur of the festival. Guests and dignitaries, including Tonare and Posidius, occupied adjacent sections. The sun dipped further, painting the sky with tints of orange and pink. The amphitheatre seemed to hold its breath, anticipating the words of the monarch. He extended his arm, a gesture inviting Esevia to share in the limelight. With grace and poise, she rose to her feet, looking at the crowd with her enchanting blue eyes that sometimes held a hint of grey, mirroring the ever-changing colours of the Bacrean Sea.

Her voice, soft yet commanding, filled the amphitheatre as she began her speech. "Citizens of Bacrea and honoured guests," she began, glimpsing quickly at Tonare. "Today we gather to honour Byra. We ask that she bless our lands with bountiful harvests and prosperity." The crowd listened attentively, the amphitheatre a sea of eager faces. Esevia continued, "In this beautiful city of Shaara, we celebrate the strength of our people and the legacy we strive to leave for generations to come." She paused, allowing her words to resonate, her gaze subtly affirming the whispered comparisons of her to Byra, embracing the role of the goddess's embodiment in her poised and elegant demeanour. She concluded, "May the grace of Byra guide us, may our endeavours be met with abundance and fulfilment.... Aternum!"

The crowd erupted into applause; the resonance echoing through the amphitheatre like a jubilant wave. King Sharadin acknowledged the crowd with a dignified nod, expressing his gratitude for their presence. As the sun sank below the horizon, the amphitheatre transformed into a canvas of cultural performances. Dancers gracefully depicted tales of fertility and harvest, their movements mirroring the cycle of nature. Musicians played melodies that seemed to transcend mortal boundaries. The primarch, Tanitos, walked slightly stooped, his steps burden by age and arthritis. His shrunken frame did little to dampen the respect his aura commanded. He approached the royal section of the amphitheatre, his steps unhurried. A cane supported his frame, a loyal companion to ease the ache of time. He descended slowly next to the monarch, the joints in his knees protesting slightly. The discomfort was apparent. Tanitos, now seated, leaned slightly towards the king, his voice carrying the weight of experience. His hands trembled slightly as he adjusted his grip on his cane. "Autokrator," he began, his voice a low straining rumble. "There are murmurs among the court that question supporting Tonare's claim to the Ahdian throne."

King Sharadin listened; his thoughtful expression illuminated by the flickering firelight. The distant tinkle of lyres blended with the scent of burning cedarwood from nearby torches. "Continue Tanitos, I know that is not all," he urged.

"Some members of the court believe it may be a better military strategy to ally with Ahdia while Kozin still rules," Tanitos continued, his eyes squinting under knitted brows. "His military experience would be beneficial to us."

Sharadin's visage remained pensive. He recognised the strategic merits of such an alliance, but also the uncertainties it posed. "There are no guarantees in matters of the throne or war," he replied, his tone reflective. "Kozin's days wane, much like my own. If an alliance were forged and he were to pass during its tenure, we would be bound to Ahdia under a ruler whose experience in war remains untested."

Tanitos nodded slowly, acknowledging King Sharadin's wisdom. "Indeed, Kozin the younger, does not possess his father's experience. And if Tonare were to ascend the throne with our support, we would have a king in our debt – a king with a desire to maintain strong relations with Bacrea." A thoughtful silence fell between them, punctuated only by the occasional pop and crackle of the amphitheatre's fire pits and the muted conversations of the attendees enveloped in the night's tepid air. Each lost in their thoughts amidst the lively performances unfolding before them.

King Sharadin finally broke the silence, his eyes still focused on the unfolding festivities. "There is much to consider," the king said thoughtfully. "Ellisar's actions will have some say in how we proceed. If he is hungry for my land in Copia, then he will ignite war soon. Then, of course, Kozin Salvator will be the ally we need."

"Yes," Tanitos replied, eyeing the side of the king's face before he went further. "Unless another path is explored."

"You speak of diplomacy," Sharadin said, shaking his head. "Paterocles thinks this is possible. While I appreciate his intentions, he does not know E'del's Successors. The boy is naïve."

Tanitos thought about voicing an explanation from Paterocles' point of view. But refrained in the end.

"Let us cast such things from thought," Sharadin said. "Tonight, I prefer the solace of wine and distraction – things that, at least, hold a promise of enjoyment."

Tanitos nodded in acquiescence, understanding the desire to momentarily escape the intricacies of ruling a kingdom. "As you wish, Autokrator. Wine and distraction shall fill the night." Their exchange concluded; they both allowed the festivities to envelop them once more. The king demanded that Tanitos partake in wine, he protested, reminding the king that he's not the man he used to be. A mere sip might rob him of his senses. But his protest was unsuccessful. No one lets the king drink alone. The atmosphere, infused with music and dance, momentarily whisked them away from the burdens of statecraft. Tonight, amid celebration, shadows of potential decisions danced in the periphery of their consciousness. As the festivities in the amphitheatre wound down, the energy in the air took on a mellower quality. The last performances had enthralled the audience, leaving them with a sense of wonder and enchantment.

Prince Tonare found a moment of reprieve. His eyes, laden with contemplation, scanned the amphitheatre, taking in the ebbing merriment. That was when his gaze met the welcoming aura of his sister, Nulynia. She approached him with a radiant smile, her aura light and welcoming. The affection he held for her was genuine, one of the few genuine connections he had in this intricate web of power and ambition.

"Nulynia," Tonare greeted her warmly, a genuine smile gracing his lips. Of all his siblings, she was the one he held closest to his heart. Her outlook on the world a beacon of happiness and perhaps a touch of naivety. He sometimes wished he could share in her carefree disposition.

"Tonare," Nulynia replied with a warm smile, her eyes alight with joy at seeing her brother. "Apologies, dear brother. I have seen little of you since your arrival."

"No need for apology dear sister, how do your children fare this day?" Tonare answered, his voice reflecting sincerity. He couldn't help but harbour a twinge of envy for Nulynia's uncomplicated happiness. The golden glow of twilight bathed the amphitheatre. Their conversation flowed, polite and measured, as they exchanged pleasantries and discussed the festivities. Nulynia mentioned her absence from the agora earlier, citing a minor ailment. Tonare could sense her genuineness, her innocence a stark contrast to the web of politics he found himself entangled in.

Then, with a touch of trepidation, "She stares on occasion," Nulynia whispered. In her eyes a hint of worry, "The envy is for my children…"

Tonare's brow furrowed, his eyes squinted slightly. However, before he could probe further, Paterocles joined them. His red hair a fiery crown, a clean-shaven face accompanied a supreme posture.

"Tonare," Paterocles interrupted, his tone polite. "May I borrow Nulynia for a moment... Will you be observing the forest rites?"

Tonare nodded. The weight of his plan and the looming spectre of his ambitions often left him with conflicting emotions. He watched as they moved away, Nulynia's laughter mingling with Paterocles' comforting presence. As they departed, Tonare couldn't help but wrestle with his conscience. He yearned for the simplicity of Nulynia's world, devoid of the burdens of ambition and hidden intentions. He hated the desires that propelled him, the need to be recognised. Seeing Nulynia's happiness and knowing that Paterocles was a good portion of that sum had him questioning his resolve. Yet, in the depths of his being, he found a way to compartmentalise and justify. Necessity, he assured himself. The path he embarked upon was always going to be fraught with moral uncertainties, but for now, Tonare suppressed his guilt and embraced the shadows that his ambitions cast upon him.

3

The gathering transitioned towards the forest edge to partake in the fertility ritual. Twilight cast a subtle enchantment upon the crowd. The amphitheatre exhaled its audience, seats emptying like whispers into the night. A diverse congregation made their way to the woodland, guided by the torchlight carried by the priesthood. The atmosphere overflowing with reverence, a hum of excitement and solemnity in the air. As the forest beckoned, they advanced in a procession, with each step taking them closer to the sacred ritual. The torches that the priesthood carried illuminated the forging dusk. Upon reaching the designated area, the priesthood orchestrated the proceedings. A deeply revered tradition to honour Byra and seek her blessings for fertility. The women of purity stepped forward to take part in the ceremony. These women were young women who had not seen more than 25 years, their eyes filled with a blend of trepidation and devotion. Their chests pulsating with belief in the goddess, each one had preserved her chastity, for the ritual held the sanctity of pure intentions. Torchlight flickered against the darkness. Tonare's gaze scanned the gathering. He noticed a familiar face - standing among the nobles and dignitaries was the shy servant girl from the Council Chamber. Swallowed up by the excitement of the festivities, he didn't notice her attending to the royal family. But he noticed her now, particularly that she stood near Queen Esevia. No, it was the way she stood in the Queen's presence. Tonare pondered amid the ritual, asking himself how he missed this before. He had been here for one year. Though, the servant girl had this eerie ability to go unnoticed – a whisper in a crowded room. A notion then materialised in Tonare's mind; a seed that germinated instantly.

A total of seven women stepped forward, one short of the required number for the ritual to be carried out. A moment of uncertainty during an otherwise seamless ceremony. Tonare saw the opportunity for his thoughts to become flesh. Posidius watched him approached the king, having no idea of his mind. Tonare moved past the bodies in front of him until he was close to the king. He leaned close to King Sharadin, his voice a discreet murmur, "Autokrator, there is a solution I can offer. Judging by appearance, the servant near your wife still has her chaste. I think she would be perfect for honouring Byra." King Sharadin turned his eyes, her innocence and unassuming nature captivating his attention.

Queen Esevia figured the intentions from the king's gazed. She protested, "No, my love. Ophelia's chaste is something I have been keeping in case of favour."

"Do you have another to put forth?" King Sharadin asked, his words becoming raw because of wine. "It seems some of the women are frightened by such an act of devotion, or perhaps the city is producing more whores." A small laughter emerged from him, something encouraged by the mirth of wine. King Sharadin started making his way towards Ophelia.

Queen Esevia voiced a last objection to the servant girl's participation in the ritual. "She possesses a certain allure... Many men of influence find that enchanting." She added in a low tone and through gritted teeth, "She is not your common slave."

She was ignored. The shy servant girl, Ophelia, stood amid the regal couple. Queen Esevia, who had attempted to form words, found King Sharadin's index finger pressed gently against her lips, silencing her. Ophelia's heart raced as she watched the monarchs with wide, uncertain eyes, her modest attire in stark contrast to the regal splendour that surrounded her. Sharadin regarded the servant girl with analytical eyes for a moment. His voice, when he finally spoke, held the weight of authority, and his question sounded more like a command to Ophelia's ears. "Would you honour Byra with your purity this night?" he asked. Ophelia, though intimidated by the moment, felt a sense of reverence and duty as she contemplated.

"Yes... I will, Autokrator." Ophelia replied, her voice laced with a nervous tremor.

The ritual was ready to begin. Eight women stood before the congregation. The priesthood began the solemn process of removing their garments, preparing them for the sacred ceremony. Vibrant paint applied to their bodies. Among the women, Ophelia stood out in her nakedness, her bashfulness and self-consciousness clear in her demeanour. Tonare approached the king once more.

"Autokrator," Tonare began, "I humbly request to partake in this ritual. It would bring me joy to honour Otia in a foreign land, and to express my gratitude to the realm of Bacrea for its hospitality." He wore a mask of reverence and gratitude, one he hoped would guard his true intentions.

King Sharadin stood watching the proceedings, his features became lined with consideration. He nodded in approval, influenced by the warmth of wine and in acknowledgement of the prince's sincere gratitude. "You have shown... great respect for our customs and traditions, Prince Tonare. You have my blessing to pay homage to Byra and Bacrea." Tonare smiled with delight.

The women stood on the threshold of the forest, ready to commence the ritual. Ophelia, her skin glazed in a soft shade of yellow, mirroring the petals of a delicate daffodil. Her nakedness accentuated by the paints tone. The eight women, a living canvas of vivid hues, awaited the moment to embark into the forest. The paint on their flesh was an embodiment of the spectrum of life, from the vibrancy of nature to the fleeting beauty of flowers in bloom. When the priest gave the command, the women ventured into the forest. With all the enthusiasm of a young deer, their bare feet carried them – a head start granted to prey over predators. Their brilliant colours soon faded into the embrace of the forest's darkness, consumed by the shadowed expanse.

Prince Tonare stood at the forefront of the congregation. He wore a flowing robe made of fine silk in deep indigo, an ode to the Koziniac Dynasty of Ahdia. The robe flowed like a midnight stream, contrasting with the tunic-clad men who were chosen next. The priesthood, guardians of tradition and ceremony, selected the remaining seven men. To be eligible, they must not have a family of their own, a condition essential to maintaining the sanctity of the ritual. In a moment charged with anticipation, the priesthood gave the order for the men to venture into the forest, seeking the women whose vibrant forms had disappeared into the night's embrace.

Tonare, his senses attuned to the forest's aura, hurried into the blackness. The forest loomed with a mysterious beauty, an intricate maze of shadows and scents. The air was heavy with the earthy fragrance of leaves and moss, and the symphony of insects and night creatures serenaded the seekers. Navigating the forest was no simple task in the absence of the sun's blessing. Tonare carefully wove through the thicket, using whatever little moonlight filtered through the canopy to guide his way. He was conscious of each sound, each rustle, each change in the night's atmosphere. In the obsidian blanket, his eyes sought the ephemeral yellow. There existed no certainty in his steps. He could draw nearer or farther from the daffodil. As he delved deeper into the forest's heart, his senses were even more challenged. In his peripheral vision, a sudden flash of turquoise caught his eye – a woman attempting to get his attention. With an air of apprehension, she emerged from behind the dense foliage. She did not hide, and Tonare's royal position was responsible for evoking this action. She wanted him, but he refused her and continued his search.

With each passing moment, the night enveloped him further. He could feel his impatient nature scratching at him - he was going to succumb to frustration.

"Sanoma's cock," Tonare whispered in the darkness. All his manoeuvring would have been for nothing if one of the other men found the daffodil first. The forest was a labyrinthine tapestry and Tonare was feeling lost in it. He saw this being much easier in his imagination. Nevertheless, the search resumed. He attempted to stifle his frustration as he went on. The vivid colours of the women's painted bodies seemed to blend into the enigmatic darkness, and the elusive yellow figure he sought remained maddeningly out of reach. The night had cloaked the forest in an impenetrable shroud, and he had doubted whether he would ever find the daffodil. Then, as he rounded a tangle of foliage, his eyes glimpsed a stain of yellow that stood out against the shades of the forest. Ophelia, her paint still vibrant in the moonlight's delicate touch, was near to him. Her presence, unexpected and hidden, stirred a wave of relief in Tonare.

Ophelia, shrouded by the thick underbrush, seemed taken aback as she noticed Prince Tonare approaching. She had likely not expected royalty to be taking part in the sacred ritual. Her body language was frigid, her surprise and unease apparent in her stance.

Tonare, conscious of her demeanour, approached her with caution. "Ophelia... is that correct?" he spoke gently. She nodded in response. "I have seen you in the palace," he continued, his eyes never leaving her. "This night is the first time I have seen you so close to the Queen. Perhaps there have been other moments, but you can be imperceptible. Tell me, do you attend Queen Esevia?"

Ophelia's response was hesitant, but truthful. "Sometimes, Excelletem. Though I tend to the needs of the palace, mostly."

Tonare probed further, his tone laced with a compassion that was untrue. "Are you a free woman serving in the palace, or are you bound by the chains of servitude?"

"I am a slave, Excelletem." Her response carried a note of resignation.

Tonare, aware of the potential leverage this information held, used it to appeal to her desire for freedom. "What if you could be free?" he said earnestly. "Not just free, but hold position and purpose." He saw Ophelia's yearning for freedom and her hesitance to trust him.

"Excelletem. How would such a thing be possible?" Confusion existed in her voice.

With gentle persuasion, he continued, "I could make it possible, once I hold greater influence in Bacrea. If you would act as my eyes and ears around Queen Esevia." He was confident about asking her this. He thought her slave status made it unlikely for her to have strong loyalties to the Queen. Then she began to shake her head swiftly. Her fear was taking hold. Tonare knew he had to seize the moment, like a fisherman trying to keep a fish on the hook.

"Ophelia," Tonare said, the earnestness in his voice compelling her to listen. "Cast aside your fear. This moment may never present itself again... and you will live and die as you are." Those words planted themselves in her mind; even with her meek ambition, that prospect was unsettling. Though that reality didn't cause this effect before, but now the carrot of freedom was being dangled before her. Ophelia had many questions, but she was thinking they weren't important.

"Position and purpose," Ophelia confirmed. For a moment, her shy eyes flickered with a flame of desire. Tonare nodded with a satisfied smile. They had reached an agreement. The prince turned his back ready to leave. This prompted Ophelia to speak. "Where do you go?" the question puzzled Tonare, so much so he didn't give a reply. Just as he was about to take another step, he felt a hand grab his wrist. Ophelia, no longer covering her chest with a shy pose, instead she held onto him.

"Wha–"

"You must have me," Ophelia pleaded, her words escaping her lips before she realised them, and she swiftly grew terribly bashful. Tonare removed her hand, but didn't proceed to leave straight away. He stared at her supple breast. His eyes traced downward, finding a thick and lush garden, where nature's verdant veil concealed her intimate mysteries. Ophelia, still bashful, felt the need to explain, "Excelletem, I do not say this because of my desires. But I wish not to receive curses from Byra."

Tonare understood.

Ophelia pleaded once more, "You must have me."

4

Prince Tonare made his way through the hallowed streets of the royal district. He walked in the stillness, the dead of night, when the world slumbered under a shroud of darkness. The moon was a silver coin in the sky, casting a gentle light upon the cobblestone. The silence was palpable. Tonare grappled with the burden of his aspirations.

The Ahdian throne, an elusive dream that had lingered in the recesses of his heart, seemed both a guiding light and a burden. He pondered the genesis of his desire for the throne, tracing it back to the influence of his father, King Kozin. His desire for the throne had been instilled in him from the earliest days of his youth. The concept of the throne had become so deeply woven into his identity that he questioned who he was without it. Tonare's garb was embellished with gold bracelets that jingled softly with each step and a striking gold necklace. He was clutching at its sistrum amulet.

His thoughts, however, took an unexpected turn. Amidst contemplations of succession and identity, he found himself thinking of Ophelia. In the night's solitude, the memory of her emerged, surprising him with its presence. Her image unfurled in his mind like delicate petals, each detail etched with clarity. He envisioned the vulnerability in her eyes, and the hesitance in her movements. The sensations came back to his mind. He could feel the warmth and delicate curve of Ophelia's thighs – a sanctuary of softness and vulnerability. It was a vision that whispered of tender secrets, a place where gentleness and hesitance intertwined in an intimate dance. How could a slave possess such a powerful nature? That the memory of it could infiltrate his mind so easily. Tonare approached the Byronaum, the sacred temple dedicated to Byra. His inner monologue was now a quiet plea for guidance from the deity. As Tonare drew nearer to the temple's exterior, he witnessed the august form emerging from the shadows. The outer walls of the temple, composed of polished marble, reflected the moonlight with a brilliant sheen. Its circular form was apparent and seeming to convey a sense of perpetuity. Perhaps an ode to certain continuities – nature of life, seasons, and the cosmos.

As he stepped into the temple, a sense of profound serenity swathed Tonare. The oculus, a circular opening at the apex of the temple's dome, permitted the moonlight to fall upon the central chamber. Tonare observed a silvery glow. The light, as if guided by the divine hand of Otia herself. Tonare's steps echoed softly as he advanced toward the central altar, his eyes keen on the scene that unfolded before him. Queen Esevia knelt before the altar in prayer. Otia had guided him once again, it seemed. He had been meaning to approach his half-sister but required it to be in private, and now Otia had presented the opportunity. But before he broached the subject with the queen, he must first offer thanks and seek further guidance from Otia.

He knelt and prayed. Nulynia was heavily on his mind; from the depths of his being, a beast pounced, his conscience compelling him to confess, and so he did. In the solemnness, under Otia's light, he admitted he would wear a crown no matter the cost. Tonare then rose to his feet. Queen Esevia mirrored his action. He glanced at the figure of Sanoma, the male deity that accompanied Byra in the temple, a deity that carried his father's features.

Queen Esevia spoke first, "I hear it will not be long before my brother is on the throne." Her delicate fingers reached for a censer holding fragrant incense, a subtle offering to the deities.

"By Otia's grace, father will yield to Egrosian tradition," Tonare expressed some optimism.

Esevia stared at the soft tendrils of smoke, curling and swirling into the air. Her eyes had not yet fallen upon Tonare. "You mistake me brother, I speak of Kozin the younger," her mockery revealed. The smile faded from Tonare's face. He was somewhat embarrassed. He shouldn't have expected any measure of kindness from her. The Queen continued, "It seems attaching yourself to my husband's realm has not increased your chances at becoming king."

Tonare strode toward the marble benches, his exterior suggesting he felt the impact of Esevia's words. He took a seat and crossed his legs. "I will do my best to increase those chances," Tonare replied. His exterior was now holding pretence, his face impassive, an effort to not give the shark before him a scent of blood.

Queen Esevia, cloaked in the hushed serenity of the temple, gracefully paced around the circular altar, swinging the censer in her delicate hand. The soft echoes of her melodic voice resonating through the sacred chamber, as she murmured the ancient hymn 'Glorious Byra'. The harmony seemed to resonate with the temple's very stones. As she circled the altar, Queen Esevia broke the sacred hymn to address Tonare. "You would do anything for the throne?" her question rhetorical, "You would present arse for fucking."

Tonare maintained a façade of impassivity. "Perhaps," he replied. He unfolded his legs and sat on the bench's edge. The prince's eyes teemed with scrutiny. He offered his analysis. "You and I may only share half-blood. Yet we are more alike than we care to confess." Tonare looked down as he absently fiddled with the gold accents on his wrist. When his eyes returned to Esevia, he noticed she had not yet met his gaze. "Your marriage to King Sharadin was not about father's diplomacy." He continued, "It was about that seed he planted within us." His impassivity remained, but emotions were trickling through these words. "We have a hunger for power... marrying Sharadin did not quench this, did it?" Tonare's gaze remained unwaveringly fixed on the queen, as though he stood at her side, his presence so palpable it seemed as if his face pressed intimately against the side of hers. He concluded, "You are a consort. You have the power to drain the royal balls... Your power is no greater than a whore's." Their gazes locked beneath the celestial radiance. Esevia's features were an illusion of stoicism. And there it was, a subtle, yet perceptible change coursed through the queen's demeanour. Emotion flickered across her eyes – a storm veiled by the tranquil moonlight – exposing the cracks in the armour she wore against Tonare's biting assessment. "You want Folger on the throne. You want him to have that very thing you have always wanted."

"I do not know what you speak of," Esevia denied.

"You do not fool me!" Tonare said strongly. His impatience seeping through, his tone caused Queen Esevia to freeze momentarily under the moonlight. He then attempted to add some levity by smiling, offering a pretentious bow before he said, "Autokratia."

"It is natural for any mother to have such wishes for her child," Esevia responded in defence. The rhythmic swinging halted under her delicate control;

43

the censer put to rest. Briefly, her gaze landed on Tonare, perhaps searching for a sign that her denial might sway him. But, as their eyes briefly locked, the unyielding scepticism etched across Tonare's features told a different story. Understanding that Tonare remained unconvinced, Esevia's composure shifted, her posture straightening as she confronted him. "What concern is it of yours, if I want these things?" she retorted, her voice echoing within the hallowed space. The circular altar seemed to bear witness to their verbal sparring.

Tonare, leaning forward on the marble bench, met her challenge with a sharp gaze. "What if I could aid in bringing such desires to life?"

Surprisingly to both, a genuine laughter escaped Queen Esevia's lips. Tonare's proposition surprised her. "Why would you do such a thing... because I am your favourite half-sister?" she said, sarcasm flowing through her words. "You do not fool me... Brother." Queen Esevia turned from him and began libation at the altar, muttering, "So Bacrea will continue to have the finest wine of all lands." The liquid offering trickled over the stone, a symbolic gesture hoping Byra will continue to bestow blessings on the fields of Bacrea.

Tonare, the golden accents on his attire softly jingling, left the marble bench. Remaining in the shadowed part of the temple, he refrained from stepping into the celestial light surrounding the altar. As Esevia poured wine on the sacred stone, Tonare spoke, his voice carrying through the sanctum. "I do not attempt to fool you. In another life, we could have been the closest of siblings. In helping Folger to the throne, I would want command over a good portion of the army." Queen Esevia looked at him with a mix of confusion and suspicion, her eyes accusing him of potentially usurping the very person he aimed to help succeed. Feeling compelled to clarify, Tonare continued, "There will be more wars, more land to take. With military command, I could forge my own kingdom."

Queen Esevia's fair hair caught the silvery embrace of moonlight as she turned to face Tonare, a jug of wine cradled in her hands. As she looked at him, the realisation dawned. "Was this always your intention?" she questioned, her voice carrying a blend of astonishment and inquiry. Tonare's quietude spoke volumes, confirming her suspicions. He then stepped onto the circular altar, bathed in the ethereal glow, his dark blonde hair tied back, and the gentle gleam of gold accents accentuating his presence. Esevia, still holding the jug of wine, asked, "What makes you think I would need your aid in achieving such desires?"

Tonare met her gaze with unflinching confidence. "You need to maintain an appearance of innocence in the court. Suspicion would fall at your feet first." He paused for a moment. "You lack the conviction. I would wager you have broached the subject with the king before, asking for some kind of competency test to see which son is more befitting of succession. Yet, my guess is that he remains unmoved by your pleas." Tonare's guesswork landed with accuracy. There wasn't a façade Esevia could conjure. Looking into the bluish grey eyes that many have compared to the Bacrean Sea, Tonare determined his words weren't enough. "Go to your husband with the matter again. See if he voices a different reply. But the king's days are not long, and soon there will be no one to ask for consideration."

As Tonare departed the sacred space, Queen Esevia watched him go, her mind a tempest of thoughts. The jug of wine in her hands felt heavier, as did the pressure of her ambitions. Tonare's analysis of the court dynamics left Esevia to ponder her next move. Observing Tonare's departure, her keen eyes curiously caught the blemishes of yellow paint on his garb. The vibrant hue, stark against the dark fabric. A subtle smile played on Esevia's lips. The Byronaum stood witness to the unfolding machinations of power and desire.

HEAD OF FIRE

284 BM

1

An untroubled stillness filled the air, only to be disturbed by the gentle rustling of fabric as Paterocles stirred from his slumber. He opened his eyes, and his gaze immediately found its way to the two tiny figures nestled beside him. The first light of dawn filtered through the sheer curtains, casting a soft glow on the ornate furnishings. Nulynia, with her flowing caramel hair covering the pillow, held their sons close. The morning sunlight coloured a delicate warmth on her serene face as she slept. They encouraged Paterocles to smile, softening the contemplative lines on his face with a tender expression. His sons, Paceros and Niranos, lay in peaceful repose, their innocence clear even in sleep. Quietly rising from the bed, Paterocles stood for a moment, silently observing the tableau of his family. It was a scene that filled him with a sense of purpose. He gently kissed Nulynia's forehead, the gesture imbued with a deep affection that needed no words. He took a final glance at his slumbering children before he turned to face the day.

The servants of the house, moving with practiced efficiency, awaited his presence. They attended to him, their hands skilful and respectful. Clothed in a rich red tunic, with leather-strapped sandals, and vambraces clasped around his forearms, Paterocles eagerly anticipated the training ahead. The final touch came as they handed him his training sword, its blade sheathed in a dark brown scabbard.

Exiting the royal estate, Paterocles found himself greeted by the embrace of the early morning mist. The verdant plain that surrounded the countryside estate was a carpet of dew-kissed grass. The untouched beauty of nature stared back at him. As the estate perched on high ground, he gazed upon the rolling hills and meadows stretching beneath him, a canvas painted in shades of green. In the distance, the capital city of Shaara emerged through the dissipating mist, its acropolis crowned with the stately propylaeum and the grand palace standing as a sentinel of authority. Paterocles stood still for a moment, his eyes capturing the familiar landmarks. Thoughts of the Fourth War of the Successors came into his mind. An important brush stroke on the canvas of his memories, twelve years old, he was when that conflict began. Eight-teen by the time it concluded. The consequences of war are often subdued by heroic tales, those with authority often speak of it in glorious terms. A soldier, just a pawn to aid the throne in acquiring victory. Not much is heard from the denizens, to who that soldier was: a father, brother, husband... friend.

Paterocles navigated the corridors of his mind like a solitary wanderer. A servant who approached with his horse interrupted his thoughts. The servant, covered in humble attire that bore the stains of diligent work, offered a deferential bow.

"Excelletem," the servant said. His eyes filled with a mix of eagerness and reverence. While he approached the prince, the horse gradually became restive. It danced nervously on its hooves. The servant grappled with the reins, desperately attempting to rein in the restless horse. He struggled to control the horse, apologising profusely for the creature's skittish behaviour. Paterocles, sensing the escalating anxiety in both horse and man, moved forward with a calming presence. His voice, usually resonant with authority, softened as he spoke soothing words to both the servant and the agitated horse. However, the horse's hysteria reached a climax, and in the chaos, the servant stumbled. Without hesitation, Paterocles leaped forward, interposing himself between the servant and the panicked horse. He caught the servant's arm, pulling him to safety. For a man of a slender frame, he possessed decent strength. With genuine concern, Paterocles helped the dishevelled servant to his feet, brushing off the dirt from his garments. He then spoke in low, soothing tones. He stroked the horse's mane and whispered reassurances. The servant, visibly shaken, attempted to apologise once more, but Paterocles' response was a reassuring hand on the man's shoulder. His eyes conveyed not disdain, but a shared humanity.

2

Paterocles guided his horse towards the training grounds. The powerful creature stepped without anxiety into the familiar arena. The glossy chestnut coat now gleamed, illuminated by the soft, golden rays of the awakening sun. A gust of wind tousled Paterocles' red hair, the scent of the training ground's earthy soil filling his senses.

His seasoned instructor, a paragon of swordsmanship, emerged. "Excelletem, ready to hone your skills?" he asked, a wry smile on his lips. The instructor's stance exuded a quiet confidence, a testament to the mastery hidden beneath the unassuming exterior. The rhythmic thud of hooves echoed as he dismounted, unsheathing his sword with fluid grace.

Paterocles nodded, a glint of determination in his eyes. "You have been besting me since I was a little boy, Pana. Perhaps today will be different."

"You ask too much of Byra this day," Pana said, laughing. Their blades danced in intricate patterns, a symphony of calculated strikes and elegant parries. The clash of steel against steel resonated through the air as Paterocles engaged in training. With every swing and parry, he released tension. His mind travelling towards clarity, mental fog dissipating, unveiling a landscape of clear thoughts. Of course, he did not defeat Panatherius. However, he found victory in achieving a clear and relaxed mind, one prepared for political discussions.

Panatherius concluded their swordsmanship practice. Paterocles, chest heaving with exertion, sheathed his sword. "Well-fought, Excelletem," Panatherius commended.

Paterocles, wiping sweat from his brow, offered a respectful nod. "Your guidance is invaluable, Pana. Training clears my mind."

As Paterocles continued to wipe his face and gathered his breath, Panatherius rested his hand on the prince's shoulder. Paterocles looked at Panatherius' large countenance, weathered by the winds of countless campaigns. "There is more to ruling than battles on the field. Negotiation can be a powerful weapon." Paterocles looked with intrigue, a face that said continue. "Your father has lived a lifetime of war. Negotiation, diplomacy–these are tools he wields with reluctance, if at all. No surprise to be found, as one of E'del's generals' blood and battle is all he knows." Panatherius now looked directly into the prince's eyes, conveying without words that he agreed on a diplomatic approach toward the potential war with Ellisar. This brought some comfort to Paterocles, knowing that their thoughts aligned. As a boy, Panatherius would often tell him stories of war, stories not filled with heroism but death, consequences and pyrrhic victories.

The stone seats, arranged in ascending tiers, stretched around the stage, creating a vast arena that would soon become a crucible of debate. The grand amphitheatre of Shaara filled with citizens, their anticipation evident. Noble families took their place at the forefront of the amphitheatre, their expressions a blend of solemnity and pride. Among them sat the merchant nobles, a distinct class whose wealth, acquired through shrewd trade, allowed them the privilege of proximity to the ruling elite. Their seats, adorned with embroidered fabrics and luxurious cushions, bespoke their financial influence and earned favour with the monarchy. Paterocles walked with measured steps towards the centre of the amphitheatre, where the stage awaited him. His gaze swept across the crowd, acknowledging the everyday people of Bacrea. A genuine smile formed as he recognised familiar faces among the masses. He felt the sense of nervous energy that circulated like a current. His ears caught murmurs of speculation and hushed conversations. As he ascended the stage, Paterocles cast a respectful eye toward the noble families seated at the front. He wasn't too fond of their steady gaze and restrained smiles. Taking his designated seat among the court members, Paterocles felt a sense of gratitude for the shade that shielded him from the sun's relentless rays. He briefly closed his eyes, allowing the coolness to soothe the warmth on his face.

The rest of the court took their seats; King Sharadin, Tanitos, Thodoris, Mekon, the high priestess and court scribes. Darius took the stage, a scrawny figure slowly making his way to address all who were present. Despite having enough to eat, the malnourished appearance clung to him like an unwelcoming odour. He absentmindedly fiddled with his hook nose as he stepped forward to address the gathering. This wouldn't be the last time. It seemed to demand his attention often.

"Citizens, nobles, and members of the court," he spoke with a voice that quivered, the weight of time causing it to struggle. "We are gathered here today by the will of Autokrator, to discuss an important matter. A matter brought forth by Excelletem." Darius' hand discovered his nose again, an unconscious habit. His youthful days were now so far behind him, and he no longer made the grand gestures that usually followed orators. "As the rumours suggest, we face the possibility of Ellisar's forces pushing westward," Darius continued, his gaze scanning the assembled crowd. "In that event, Excelletem is proposing that we seek negotiations over war." Whispers of intrigue reverberated through the crowd; a few noble faces danced between fascination and mild shock. There were some groans at the front of the amphitheatre. Groans coming from the stage as well. Darius left centre stage, a sign for court members to begin the verbal jousting.

As the master of ceremonies retreated, Thodoris, the strategos, rose to speak. His voice cutting through the sounds of the crowd. "All faith cannot be put in rumours," Thodoris asserted, "but scouts have spotted more of Ellisar's army in the East of Copia." The babbling amongst the audience started again. Thodoris continued, undeterred by the growing unease, "We can look to a man's past actions to measure him, and Ellisar's campaigns Far East are evidence of his thirst for land." His words hung heavy in the air. The atrophic scar, inscribed across his face, underscored his dispassionate expression. A nobleman, draped in fine robes, rose eagerly from his seat at the front of the amphitheatre. Thodoris, not yet fully settled in his seat, turned his attention toward the outspoken noble.

"How long will any diplomatic solution hold such ambitions at bay?" The question hung over the crowd. His gaze fixed on Paterocles. The nobleman's raised brows and animated gestures emphasised the gravity of the inquiry, challenging Paterocles to provide a satisfactory response. "Can Excelletem speak to this?" he concluded, his tone leaving no room for ambiguity.

King Sharadin's eyes panned to his future successor.

Paterocles rose from his seat. Taking his time. A deliberate act. A wry smile on his face, he straightened his linen garment with regal red trim. He was very aware of the power of theatrics. "Seeing the future is work for gods, not men," Paterocles replied, his tone entwined with sarcasm and mockery. "*Though*," he added, drawing out the word with theatrical flair, "I am flattered that you think of me so highly." Paterocles spoke with feigned humility. Small pockets of laughter emerged in the crowd. The nobleman's face expressed his displeasure, as a face complimented by a head of fire and a diadem stare down at him.

Before Paterocles could fully retake his seat, another noble rose, his voice high pitched and demanding. "With respect, Excelletem, you avoid question."

Now more than earlier, the prince could feel all the eyes in the amphitheatre. He met his father's stare for a moment. A stare that almost dared him to expand on his point of view. Upright once again, the would-be king gathered himself to address the crowd, without theatrics and mockery. "Perhaps Ellisar will never be satisfied; that is very possible." His expression became more serious. "However, I believe his desire for more of Copia is a result of the Fourth War of the Successors." The amphitheatre listened keenly, his eyes scanning the stage, then the audience. "Whatever we think of the man," he emphasised, "his actions grabbed victory from the hands of Priam." The prince, recognising his following words would be unpopular, took a moment before he concluded. "I say, we give up some of our land in Copia, as a recognition of his work in that war. That way, we can scratch ego and quench thirst."

As Paterocles presented the audacious proposal of ceding land to Ellisar, the agitation simmered beneath the surface of the aging king. With a suddenness, King Sharadin sprang from his chair. "He did not win that war alone," He thundered, the emphasis on *alone*. Paterocles, still standing with an air of poised defiance, continued to look his father's way. "What kind of king do you think me?" King Sharadin's fingers clawed at the air, tense and quivering with the intensity of his emotions, as if he sought to strangle the words that hung between them. "Give up land because the mighty Superare wants it," King Sharadin scoffed, the contempt in his voice clear. "Spread cheeks with both hands," the king concluded, a crude metaphor along with an equally crude gesture that painted the indignity of such a submission.

Tanitos rose from his seat, his aura exuding composure. He leaned on his cane to steady himself, and then his hand found its place on King Sharadin's shoulder. The king reluctantly anchored, a rare moment of calm descending upon him. While Tanitos addressed the assembly, he specifically directed his words at the prince. "I have said before that I am not completely against war or diplomacy. However, Excelletem, there are things we must consider," he began, his eyes squinted with the scrutiny of a strategist. "Giving up land could display weakness, and what if Ellisar asks for more?"

As Tanitos posed his question, the nobleman, with the high-pitched voice, fuelled by the passion of the debate, stood abruptly. A breach of customary decorum that drew a collective gaze. "There will be blood after giving land, and the beast will come again and again," the noble proclaimed. Recognising that his actions were uncustomary, a gaze from the king helped him to identify this. The nobleman nodded in apology. The comment had now elicited a rowdy response from the noble families, their voices rising in a cacophony of concern. This concern had worked its way to the regular people in the audience. Darius, the master of ceremonies, raised his hands to quell the rising tumult. The final hushing of the masses came when Excelletem rose again to answer the questions both said and unsaid. Paterocles could imagine the possible scrutiny that swirled around present minds, the questions born from unintentional fearmongering. The sun, its warmth, an unyielding embrace, descended upon the gathered multitude. The subdued murmurs of the crowd intermingled with the distant trill of cicadas. Paterocles cast his gaze across the nobles, then turned inward to scrutinise himself, and finally, his eyes settled on the fellow court members sharing the stage. Thinking about how they, himself included, enjoyed lavish shading. His eyes fell upon the everyday people who sat in heated discomfort. *They never think of them*, he mused.

"The real question," Paterocles declared, his voice subduing murmurs, "Is how prepared are we for war and what price are we willing to pay? The 'we' I speak of are not those of us in fine robes, but those of us who sleep outside the comforts of palace walls and lush estates." With the crowd's demeanour shifting, a subtle acknowledgement emerged that, for this moment, someone considered them in the matter. A collective nod of approval rippled through the onlookers. "Fath–" he corrected himself, remembering the formalities, "Autokrator has always told me it is important to be honest about an enemy's strengths. Pride can get you killed. Ellisar has gone further east than E'del ever did. You have heard tales about men in the Far East - they invent new ways to kill a man every day. Your worst nightmares have not shown you something as barbarous."

Before the carmine headed prince could continue, the head of yet another noble family interrupted with an accusatory tone, accusing Paterocles of cowardice. The interruption disrupted the flow of words, leaving a pause that seemed to stretch uncomfortably. King Sharadin's eyes grew as the crowd exchanged uncertain glances. There was a subtle gesture. The nobleman, realising the consequences of his disdainful remarks, found himself surrounded by the imposing presence of the royal guards. The removal took place swiftly, but not without a degree of severity. They dragged him like wild game, causing his gorgeous fabrics and groomed complexion to become one with dirt. Merchant nobles observed the scene with smirks, finding joy from the traditional nobles being reminded of their limitations.

Paterocles resumed, unfazed by the brief interruption. "I wish only to be honest about the enemy and give an answer to the question: What price are we willing to pay?" His words lingered, allowing the gravity of the query to seep into the minds of those gathered. Paterocles invoked the spectre of the Fourth War of the Successors – a portrayal that allowed the audience to grasp the potential realities they might face. "Consider the

Fourth War of the Successors, which took six years to conclude – a war where three united against one powerful enemy. How long will this war last if we must fight Ellisar on our own?" The weight of his words lingered, the implications sinking into the collective consciousness of those present.

A merchant noble rose to speak. His prosperity gained through shrewd commerce rather than martial prowess. He attempted to quell his nervous, not as accustomed to the grandiosity of political discourse as the traditional nobles were. "Excelletem speaks with wisdom beyond the bounds of our city walls," the merchant noble declared, his gaze sweeping across the assembly. "The cost of war is not measured solely in lives lost in battle but extends to the economic prosperity of Bacrea. Trade, a lifeline that courses through the veins of our realm, could wither in the shadow of conflict." Traditional nobles, many of whom had ascended to their positions through feats of military valour, bristled at this perspective. They exchanged disapproving glances and muttered objections under their breaths.

King Sharadin, in a toga mirroring Paterocles' – white with red trim – rose from his seat. His gut, prominent under the toga. Sweeping his vision across the amphitheatre, the monarch's head glinted in the daylight, the crown on his head heavily encrusted with rubies. The king's gaze turned toward the High Priestess; a figure revered for her spiritual insight rather than political acuity. Sharadin, with a nod of respect, invited her to share her views – an unusual act, as it was not customary to ask another to voice their opinion while standing ready to give yours. A gesture that deviated from customary practice but went unchallenged in deference to the king's status. "High Priestess," he said, "I seek your guidance."

"I await a sign from Byra," she stated. "Only when the goddess is ready, will I provide counsel."

The king was privately sceptical. He perceived her reply as a diplomatic sidestep, but refrained from vocalising his doubts. The reverence for Byra preventing any overt challenge. Sharadin simply provided a respectful nod before he addressed the assembly. "A good military tradition provides deterrence," he declared, his passion beginning to seep through, taking the form of gestures. "It is a deterrence! That has secured our borders and kept our enemies at bay." The red trimmed robe patrolled the stage, peering into the audience, as if he sought to meet the gaze of every eye. His feet ceased for a moment as he turned his attention to Paterocles. "To surrender land would be to compromise the very security that has allowed Bacrea to prosper," King Sharadin spoke while making direct eye contact with his heir. The head of fire patrolled again. This time his eyes were searching the front of the amphitheatre. They found Myron, the merchant noble, who expressed concerns about trade amidst war. "Good Myron, you are a clever man. You know that trade flourishes under the aegis of military stability," he spoke while staring down at the noble, who returned an acquiescent nod. "I would wager," he began, resuming his patrolling, his words no longer aimed at one individual. "That there are those of you here who have some awareness of history. From the First War of the Successors to the Fourth." His gaze turned introspective, as if he sought through the sands of time. "The most trusted generals of E'del fought over his vast territory. Jealousy, ambition, a desire for a fair piece of what they helped build—these were the elements that gave life to the flames of conflict," the king's hands a cradle, holding a metaphorical flame. "Priam was the first to show a thirst for everything," he continued, a glint of reproach in his eyes. "After a few successful campaigns receiving the epi 'Superare,' we know who had that thirst next." Paterocles sat in shaded comfort, interestingly he noticed how quiet the audience was. It would be superficial to assume that the regality was the sole cause. No. It was the way he spoke, his presence on the stage. The audience engaged; their attention captured. Sharadin paced across the stage, his mainly white robes billowing with each step. "Ellisar's ultimate goal is not coexistence; it is dominance!" A resounding declaration reverberated; the conviction that oozed from the king became almost tangible. He walked back and forth with a clenched fist, a sigil of the view he held. Again, the king peered into the audience curiously, looking as if the multitude had formed one face entirely. His fist softened as he approached Paterocles' vicinity. "Ellisar's actions attest to his true desires. Treaties, agreements - they are but fleeting shadows when confronted with the ambitions of a ruler who knows no bounds," he spoke with a sudden calm while he stared deeply into the eyes of his child.

3

Seated on a stone bench, Paterocles sought solace in the palace gardens. The oppressive heat of the day had taken its toll, leaving him mentally fatigued. With a sigh, he relieved himself of the ceremonial headpiece, delicately lifting it from his head. The fine rubies embedded in the diadem glinted in the sunlight, catching his eye. His gaze fixated on the precious gems. As he cupped the fine craftsmanship, his eyes pensive, a thought perhaps long suppressed unshackled itself. *We cannot win this war.* It escaped from the depths of his mind; an air bubble desperate to reach the surface of consciousness. He couldn't deny the candid echo. Paterocles grappled with the stark reality of the statement. When he factored in his father's unyielding stance, the impending conflict became more real.

Maybe it is rumours after all. Thoughts attempted to ease anxiety. He sat with a contemplative demeanour beneath the shade of shrubs, their leaves providing a cool refuge. As he wallowed further and further into his thoughts, a voice surprised him.

"I knew you would seek shade on a day like this," she spoke with a teasing lilt in her voice, her words a gentle ribbing that carried the warmth of familiarity. Her eyes sparkled with a mix of affection and a hint of mischievousness. "I was afraid I would find you a prune." Nulynia's aura, an intense yellow that seemed to radiate positivity and vitality, enveloped her. The vibrant energy she exuded had an almost tangible effect on the atmosphere, infusing the surroundings with a renewed sense of life. As she drew closer to Paterocles, her presence became a gentle force, lifting the weight that seemed to burden him after the political debate.

"Would you still hold me close to heart, if a prune was all I was," He returned tease as he looked up at her and smiled.

"I would love you if a grain of sand was all you were," she replied, taking a seat beside him. Their laughter echoed through the palace gardens, a melody of shared joy that momentarily dispelled the heavy energy lingering in the air. Paterocles marvelled at how effortlessly Nulynia could weave warmth into the fabric of the moment. It was one of the reasons he loved her so. He could live a thousand lifetimes and still never find the words to express this to her.

"I did not expect to lay eyes upon you," Paterocles said, expressing his surprise. "I know of your heart toward..." He took a quick glimpse at the palace.

Nulynia smiled. "Yes... but I came for you," she rested her hands on top of his. "I knew the debate, along with the heat, would have your spirits low." Her touch eased any tension in Paterocles' hands, then she slowly pried the golden adornment from him. Nulynia's hand found its way to Paterocles' shoulder, after she had placed the diadem back on his head. A gesture of comfort and support. The warmth of her touch was a balm to his frustrations and worry.

Still not completely out of his own head, Paterocles, for a moment, wrestled to share the revelation that had surfaced during his contemplation. He hesitated, thinking that once he said it, it couldn't be unsaid. *What if I burden her with concern?* As she held him close, her touch carried an unspoken understanding. The tenderness in her embrace conveyed a silent promise - that they would face the challenges ahead together. He melted into her embrace like candle wax yielding to the warmth of a flame. Paterocles, feeling the calming effect of Nulynia's presence, found himself compelled to open up.

"I had a thought," he said, his expression shifting to a more serious note. "A realisation, really." He stared into her eyes. They were not like her sister's; they carried the blue of the sky. Celeste. "We cannot win this war," he admitted.

Nulynia's eyes grew wide. "Tell me you did not speak this at the debate."

"Of course not," he relinquished himself from her embrace. "I am no fool, Nu."

Nulynia, driven by an instinctive need to offer comfort, sought to embrace him once more. Her arms encircled him, attempting to draw him close again. He resisted the pull back into the warmth of their shared cocoon. Exasperation was visible on his face.

"Some seem to think that we are the most powerful realm," he ranted. "But none of those foolish nobles, with all their military heritage, consider that we could be against stronger forces." His gaze shifted, scanning the idyllic beauty of the palace gardens.

As Nulynia listened, she attempted to embrace him again.

"No formal alliance with King Kozin has been made," he declared. "Even with Kozin's alliance, victory might barely be grasped, possibly leaving wounds on the realm we may never recover from." He paused, a weighty silence settling between them as he contemplated a more ominous outcome. "Without an alliance, our realm could face its demise."

Nulynia, led by anxiety, interjected, "You must find a moment to spea–"

"I have done so before, Nu." Paterocles interrupted. "His personal feelings toward the man cloud his judgement."

"I see," Nulynia said tentatively. "Grant me pardons. You know I hold no ill thoughts toward your father. But can we not simply wait for his days to end? You said before, he continues to ignore the advice of the medicus, drinking whenever he pleases. Can we not wait, then the decis–"

"We cannot be certain, Nu. We cannot be certain of the days. How many? Talks of diplomacy must be swift, the moment Ellisar makes a move that confirms war, talks of diplomacy become much harder no matter who the ruler is," Paterocles replied, his tone firm.

Nulynia took his face in her hands, gently turning his gaze to meet hers. "If your thoughts on this are correct," she began, her voice carrying a soft but unwavering tone, "You must try again." Some reluctance remained in the prince's eyes. Seeing this, Nulynia added, "For our children." In a flash the fire of determination re-emerged, Paterocles realising that the realm was bigger than him. But also bigger than his father. It was more than any man who sat next to the axe of fire. Paterocles' eyes now conveyed this resolve. It was clear for Nulynia to see, and her response was a warm smile. Nulynia slowly invaded Paterocles' personal space. The garden, a panorama of green hedges, bore witness to their intimate connection. Their mouths melded in a soft collision, a silent exchange of promises and an intimate escapism. Paterocles' lips sought solace in the warmth of Nulynia's kiss.

Charged by an undeniable passion, Nulynia poured her emotions into the kiss with a newfound intensity. Her fingers entwined in the fabric of his linen robe, pulling him closer with a fierce determination. The green verdure of the gardens observed this unexpected surge of desire. Her passion was contagious. Paterocles surrendered to the escalating intimacy, reciprocating Nulynia's fervour. Then she broke the kiss abruptly and stood before him.

Paterocles' heart raced with the excitement of the unexpected. The air, thick with anticipation. With every gentle movement, she held his gaze. Her perizoma, a delicate whisper between her thighs, succumbed to the gravity of her intentions. The delicate fabric yielded to her touch, sliding away like petals under the caress of a tender breeze. Throughout this silent revelation, Nulynia maintained eye contact, the windows to her soul now veiled with a different kind of vulnerability.

Words dared not intrude.

Closing the distance between them, Nulynia positioned herself in a straddle before retrieving his manhood. As he entered her universe, her grip on him tightened. A gasp escaped from her. A squelch resonated in the air, and with each passing moment as she took him in more and more, the sound transformed into a wetter, soppier noise. The waters of her universe flowed down his trunk. The walls of her universe dripped, legs quivered, besieged by the gentle onslaught of Paterocles' firm affections. They were both going to reach the zenith. Her eyes pleaded with a silent intensity, to not stop, but Paterocles had reached the ceiling of his virility. With great effort, the prince held on for a few more moments, and Nulynia's universe exploded. The uncontrollable tremble took her whole being, but was dominant in her legs. Paterocles relaxed, nearly falling off the stone bench as he gave seed.

4

"Sanoma's cock!" In the dimly lit Royal Study room, King Sharadin sat alone. Seated at his grand wooden desk, he found no victory in the daunting pages of the *New Tongue* script before him. The room, bathed in the soft glow of oil lamps, felt stifling as unfamiliar characters pressed on him. The envoys from Ahdia had arrived earlier. They had already read the messages for him, perhaps informed of the king's inability before arrival.

However, the king was determined to grasp the written form for personal understanding and verification. His struggle stemmed from various factors. Sharadin had limited exposure to the New Tongue in written form, but it was extensively used in Ahdia. His late introduction to the art of writing also contributed to his deficiency. He could just about read and write in the language of his homeland, Gelare. The Ahdians had applied one of their alphabets to the language of Gelare – Patin. Under subjugation, once E'del conquered, they used the same alphabet to create a new language to aid in assimilation. That language was the *New Tongue*. Both languages may share the same visual symbols, but their arrangement and phonetic values differ. The administrative practices across his vast realm, spanning from Bacrea to Gelare and West of Copia, saw official records kept in Patin. This also aided in the rift in his understanding.

King Sharadin squinted at the scrolls, finding the letters on the papyri dancing and shifting as if with a life of their own. He grumbled in frustration, taking another sip of wine. He knew well that the wine wasn't enhancing his mental capacities. Yet, he had consumed too many cups to retreat now. On the corner of his desk, a small bronze figurine caught the flickering light. It depicted the male deity Yius, a synthesis of Kozin's composite deity Sanoma and the cultural infusion of Gelare.

A low, deliberate knock pierce through the sturdy wooden door of the Royal Study, momentarily disturbing the quiet within. King Sharadin, engrossed in the scrolls spread across his grand desk, answered the disturbance with a grumble, a subtle indication of his momentary vexation.

"Father," came Paterocles' voice from the other side, revealing his identity. The door creaked open slowly, allowing the prince's figure to emerge in the doorway. An enclosed and secluded space, the Royal Study was. The faint glow within helped to create its inherent cosiness. An ambiance that felt both intimate and secure met Paterocles. The prince fully emerged from behind the sturdy door, a silent entrance dictated not by verbal invitation or gesture, but by the absence of protest against his presence. He witnessed his father perched over the deep-coloured wood grain of the wooden desk. Paterocles journeyed into the room. King Sharadin sat in loose-fitting fabrics of a gentle blue. In the dimness, Paterocles perceived garments that looked closer to grey. The prince's gaze held a curious intensity as he studied the king. He found a seat away from the grand desk, but positioned himself directly in front of it. The aged wood creaked slightly beneath his weight. Curiosity still plagued Paterocles' eyes. Though unaware of the specific subject of the scrolls, he allowed his thoughts to wander into the realm of speculation. Moments passed before Paterocles broke the silent. "Word from Clomon?" A wrinkle of concern on his brow.

King Sharadin lifted a goblet to his lips, savouring the taste as he took a contemplative sip. He lowered the goblet; he briefly lifted a scroll, presenting it for Paterocles to see. "No, these," he spoke with a laboured voice, "are not matters of the treasury." Paterocles, standing at the doorway of an intimate exchange, noted his father's deliberate avoidance of eye contact. Even the way he spoke... The prince's irritation was subtle, but began to nibble at the edges of his composure. However, he didn't give in to his irritation. He thought of what had occurred earlier that day. Perhaps a peace offering would help, an admission.

"My words at the debate about ceding land was just a possibility of negotiation," he sat crossed leg and absently fiddled with his fingers. "There could be other paths to explore." Paterocles looked up from his fingers, sincerity ran through his words. "I would never think of ceding the city of Tir–"

"I know you would never insult your mother's memory," Sharadin interjected. "The heat drove you shitwitty, but you are not completely mad."

Sharadin briefly glanced up from the scrolls. The shadows of the room played on his ageing features. Their eyes met for a split second. Paterocles caught the undertones of disapproval that lingered on his father's face. The disappointment barely veiled. Paterocles felt the bubbling inside himself, steadily raising, the urge to lash out, to question why his father seemed so willing to thrust the realm into conflict. The rational side of him knew that taking that road was unwise. He somehow found the composure to restrain the temper and delay the inevitable clash of their views. "What are the scrolls about, and why do they seem to drive you to madness?" Paterocles asked, changing the course of conversation... Momentarily.

A grumble was the initial response. The dissonant expression on the king's face revealed a mixture of frustration and irritation. Still engrossed in the contents of the scrolls, Sharadin took a moment to finish the dark liquid in his goblet, a red so deep it verged on black in the dimness. "These," gesturing toward the scrolls spread across his desk, "They are words from Ahdia. Kozin wishes to torment me, so he sends them formed in the New Tongue."

"Did the envoys not–"

"Yes, of course," Sharadin replied, "but I would like to read it for myself, to retain the details. If only he sent it in Patin."

"Ahdia is the centre for the New Tongue, and it has spread vastly," Paterocles remarked.

"Yes, he wishes to remind me of that," Sharadin said with a reflective tone. "The scrolls concern the matter of alliance."

Paterocles, sitting up with a sudden surge of optimism, couldn't help but hope for a positive turn of events. "He is willing?" he asked, knowing that an alliance, while not his first choice, would lend them confidence if war became inevitable.

"Eat your excitement, boy," Sharadin remarked dryly. "He but states his reasons he must delay. Some details escape my mind, but to simplify—he claims to have given my realm two beautiful daughters, worthy of the court, and I am yet to send him one."

"Esse should marry now," Paterocles suggested.

"Yes, yes, that is fair to point out," Sharadin agreed. "He mentions something about internal matters in his realm. Still trying to get the sacred community to accept Sanoma. His obsession with getting close to the Loom is unrivalled. Not even E'del was this determined." King Sharadin reached for a black terracotta oinochoe that sat on the cedarwood. The vessel contained scenes of the

Byronia, and King Sharadin traced the painted images with a subtle reverence. Paterocles observed his father's movement. After he had refilled his goblet, a second goblet emerged from the shadows. The prince, though not particularly desiring wine, observed the liquid pouring into the second cup, acutely aware that he couldn't decline this silent invitation. Paterocles approached the desk; he extended his hand to receive the goblet from his father. On his way back to his chair, a wry smile appeared on his lips. The dark liquid shimmered in the candlelight. He noticed the goblet brimming with wine. *I will never match him for drinking*, Paterocles thought. Yet, the medicus had warned against it; and still his father drank heavily. The prince's smile faded.

Sharadin resumed, "There is another matter of strategic importance. The specifics elude me for now, but with dawn's arrival and wine's fading influence..." He trailed off momentarily, lost in contemplation. His gaze fixed upon the goblet as if it held the key to the complexities swirling in his mind. "In any case," he continued. "There is nothing to be done about his internal issues or strategic affairs." Sharadin organised a pair of scrolls, placing them aside while leaving another in the centre of his desk. "This," he declared, gesturing toward the solitary scroll. "Is within my power to act upon. I have decided to bestow Esse upon Kozin's realm, to be wed to Kozin the younger. In Ahdia, she shall be known as Queen Esevia I, with no need for the truncation of her name."

"She is not very fond of the truncation," Paterocles chimed in.

"Yes, well, if Kozin accepts her..." He trailed off again. "I can make out some of these. This scroll is kinder, it seems." Paterocles listened intently, flicking droplets of wine from his fingers that had escaped the confines of the cup. He took a substantial gulp, possibly hoping the wine would help him speak with absent nerves. The prince was on the verge of broaching the pressing matter in his heart, yet his father pre-empted the discussion.

"Why have you sought me out this night?" Sharadin questioned. "Did you go knocking on every door until you found me?" he added with raised brows and tease in his words.

"Your wife pointed me to the right place," Paterocles replied. "Every door would be too much work for the future king," he returned tease.

Sharadin chuckled, a deep and rumbling sound that seemed to pulsate through the dimly lit study. His eyes carried a playful gleam. "Yes, I suppose my days are growing short," he admitted, his tone filled with an air of jest and contemplation. His laughter subsided, as he regarded Paterocles with a more serious expression. "Although the thoughts in your mind frighten me... How long will the realm last with you seated next to the axe?"

Paterocles felt a hurtful twinge. He met Sharadin's gaze with a steely resolve. It was the first time he had heard his father speak words of uncertainty about his succession. "Do you not think me fit to rule, father?" Paterocles inquired, his voice carrying subtle notes that exposed the wound beneath his exterior.

Sharadin, seeing the emotions on his son's face, felt a softening within. He sighed, acknowledging the weight of his words. "Of course you are, you are my thunder," he reassured, trying to alleviate the tension that had settled in the room.

But Paterocles sought unfiltered honesty. "Do not offer me pity, Father, speak the truest words," he demanded. "Do you think me a coward, like the noble–"

"If I shared the views of the nobleman, I would not have had him dragged from sight," Sharadin replied, his voice becoming elevated. Visibly irritated, Sharadin angrily put three scrolls back into tubes, the frustration obvious in his every movement. Paterocles watched him, deciding against further drinking as he put away his goblet.

"Your naivety, that is what frightens me," Sharadin declared.

Paterocles, unflustered, replied with a firm tone, "Because I seek another way? Because I think of the common people, not only in Shaara, but in the other parts of our realm?"

"Think like a king!" The room seemed to echo with Sharadin's thunderous response. His voice returned to a normal pitch as he continued, "Your empathy for commoners is admirable; you have your mother's heart. But you must think beyond them, make sacrifices they will never understand, just as you will never understand hunger or a hard day's labour." Sharadin downed the wine and threw the goblet across the room, the sound of it bouncing across the floor amplifying the gravity of his words. "You do not know men of ambition, greed, war. You do not negotiate with an enemy you believe you can defeat. Is that not why you seek negotiation?"

Paterocles' eyes widened for a fleeting moment. Those words cut through him, clean, exposing the realisation he had come to in the palace gardens. His father was aware of it long before he was, and now he sat before him, grappling with the inability to find a reply to the weighty question that lingered in the air. He opted not to let his doubts materialise into words, but the ensuing silence... A sigh escaped from Sharadin; the stillness had breathed life into Paterocles' uncertainties.

"What of your grandchildren, Paceros and Niranos? What realm will they inherit if we struggle to recover from the wounds of war?"

"Beautiful boys... Awful names," the wine now granting passage to unfiltered thoughts. "Perhaps they will possess the strength to rebuild this great realm. They can stand on historic pride, knowing their predecessors never parted cheeks in the face of a powerful adversary," Sharadin stated.

The prince smirked in the face of his father's inebriated honesty. He located the goblet he had set aside earlier and rose from his chair, emerging from the heavily shadowed section of the room. Paterocles' features, once ablaze with determination, now reflected weariness and defiance. Approaching his father, he could now perceive the blue of the fabric that decorated King Sharadin's form. The goblet was placed on the cedarwood, much wine still in its contents.

Meeting his father's gaze, Paterocles concluded the conversation with a simple acknowledgement, "Your wisdom, Father." The words carried a tone of submission. A submission that was a façade to disguise the subtle rebellion beneath. In that moment, Paterocles turned on his heel, making the conscious decision to leave the dimly lit study. As he walked away, he was resolute in his decision. The decision to contact Ellisar himself had solidified in his mind.

CHAMBER INTIMACIES

284 BM

1

The sturdy door of the Royal Study closed with a muffled thud, stifling the feeble grasp of candlelight attempting to spill into the dim corridor. King Sharadin's fingers lingered on the cold brass handle before he turned away. The hour was late, and the burdens of both statecraft and familial tensions weighed upon him. As the first echoes of his footsteps reverberated in the marble corridor, Sharadin's gait remained firm, assured by the wine that had accompanied the evening's discourse. However, with each step, the confident stride transformed into a clumsy dance. The colonnades that lined the corridor became companions that stopped him from falling. The king's movements swayed, zigzagging between the pillars.

Thoughts rolled through his mind like a cylinder object. Amid this mental motion, Sharadin realised the subtle rift that was forming between father and son. In the haze of wine-laden contemplation, the king's mind conjured fragments of an Old Gelare myth that had been embellished with the essence of Yius. The tale spoke of Lumis and Umbros, brothers birthed in divine madness. Lumis, the embodiment of light, yearned for eternal day, while Umbros, the shadowy counterpart, sought perpetual darkness. Sharadin continued to stagger through the corridors; the doors of the master bedroom felt as though they would never appear.

Lumis and Umbros, once at odds, discovered the harmony that lay in the intertwining dance of light and shadow. The myth resonated with the king's introspection, and he wondered if he and his son could find a similar harmony within their divergent views.

Sharadin moved through the dimly lit corridors like a phantom. He heard the echoing of footsteps that weren't his own. Two royal guards patrolled the dimly lit corridors. They emerged from the shadows like vigilant sentinels. Their muscular arms clasped circular shields and rested gleaming spears at the ready. A murmur of recognition passed between them before one guard took a decisive step forward. "Autokrator," he intoned, addressing King Sharadin with the required respect.

The inebriated monarch waved off the offered help. With a regal determination, Sharadin straightened himself, his posture morphing into one that commanded respect even in the throes of intoxication. His eyes, still glazed from wine, held a glint of authority as he regarded the guards. The king offered a gracious nod before he said, "*Omnis bene est*" (All is well).

The guards resumed their patrol, their disciplined strides echoing through the quiet corridors. It was no surprise to encounter the king in a state of inebriation; he had a well-known fondness for wine. Duty-bound, the guards continued their watchful march. Sharadin eventually reached the doors of his bedroom. The promise of rest and the anticipation of the sweet release of slumber hung in the air. However, awaiting him beyond the doors was not only the embrace of sleep but also his wife, Esevia.

2

The canopied bed was at the centre of the master bedroom, complimented by lavish fabrics. Queen Esevia laid upon it, her gaze fixed upon the entrance as King Sharadin strode into the room. She already knew he was drunk, whether through intuition or routine. As Sharadin approached the wooden furniture, he delicately removed his rings, placing them thoughtfully upon the surface. The faint clink of metal on wood echoed. Her eyes lingered on his dark red locks, marvelling at their resilience against the passage of time. They defied the encroaching touch of grey, keeping vibrancy.

Memories stirred. She reminisced about their union, a man of sixty years he was when they wed. To her surprise, he surpassed her expectations. Sharadin, even in his sixtieth year, retained a magnetic allure. The pull extended beyond physical attributes; it was an amalgamation of experience, strength, and charm. Once a burlier man, he now carried a different form. Her thoughts traced the contours of his figure, recognising the changes time had made. But she thought he carried them well. Confidence does much for a man.

Sharadin stood, his attention fixated on his fingers now liberated from the rings that had encircled them. It was peculiar, the contemplation on his face. Although now, perhaps the wine was staring for him.

A low tone from the bed, "What is it?"

"I will have these melted and re-crafted," Sharadin asserted.

Esevia, propped up on her elbow, held an inquisitive look. "You desire a new appearance?"

"No," Sharadin replied, still engaged with his hands. "My fingers are getting fat."

Esevia stifled a laugh, her eyes gleaming with a mischievous spark. With a feigned seriousness, she responded, "Stubby fingers can be useful tools." The innuendo was not lost on him.

King Sharadin turned his attention to his last pieces of jewellery – the gold bracers encircling his wrists. The subtle sound of metal meeting wood accompanied each delicate movement as he removed them. He chose not the bed, with its rich drapery cascading from the intricately carved canopy, but another seat in the chamber. The ebb and flow of alcohol in his veins manifested in a returning clumsiness to his gait. He seated himself; the act infused with a heavy exhale. As he regarded his queen, his eyes focused on a soft detail - the subtle pinkness of her nipples caught his attention. It stared at him.

She still gently propped her form on an elbow. A long, delicate robe of pink mesh barely clothed her. The fabric seemed almost an extension of her grace, subtly revealing the lines that made whispers among the people linger–the suggestion that she might be the human embodiment of Byra herself. Sharadin followed the lines of her figure. Now that he wasn't engrossed in his hands, he recognised the smoothness of her skin, which prompted a realisation. Esevia had indulged in a milk bath. The subtle fragrance that lingered caught his attention.

There could be only one reason she would wear such a rare and expensive spice, Sharadin thought. The air carried the aromatic whispers of saffron. Sharadin found the evolution of their union intriguing – a union born not out of a father's diplomatic manoeuvrings but orchestrated by the hands of a daughter. His wife had gone to the plains of the afterlife two years prior, leaving him a widower. The prospect of a new union with Kozin's daughter wasn't one that filled him with unbridled joy, but it bore the weight of political foresight. He could see only pluses for the realm. The surprise lingered in his reflections; she, a young woman, willingly embracing marriage to a man who exceeded her by many years. Perhaps it was the naivety of youth that led her to accept this union, underestimating the gravity of the duties that came with it or harbouring expectations of obtaining a measure of power through co-regency. He would say it was the latter.

"Sharadin, my love," Esevia said. She sat up in the bed. Few people could address him so. She continued, "There is something I wish for you to give consideration," hesitance in her voice.

"Sounds like something that requires much mental energy," Sharadin stated. His voice carried the warmth of wine-induced ease. "I am afraid... I am in the hands of wine. My mind can only consider sleep."

Esevia pressed on, flashing a teasing smile. "You and I both know you could drink a city dry and still discuss the most complex of politics." The amusement then faded from her face as she added in a more serious tone, "Speaking of, do you intend to hasten your journey to the afterlife?"

"I take the recommended herbs, Esevia," he said, his face tightening with annoyance. "But I will never part with wine." Sharadin rustled in his chair, his inner monologue reluctantly acknowledging her concern. In recent times, his once formidable tolerance for wine was fading.

The queen went back to the matter of consideration, knowing she couldn't circumvent his stubbornness toward drinking.

Consideration? Her presentation does not suggest conversation, Sharadin mused.

Esevia, noting the king's tacit acknowledgement of her words, continued. "I want you to consider Folger for the throne."

...In the silence that followed, Sharadin's thoughts swirled. *All these fools wish to talk this night... Mmm, does she wish to manipulate me with her appearance? No, she is wiser than that. Her intentions to seduce me are genuine, but in the presence of that, she wishes to weave in her plea.* The king escaped the walls of his mind to voice words, "Esevia," he began, his head leaning on his fist. "Have we not had this discussion before... Folger, is my son... but he is not the thunder of my loins."

"Why must we stick to the ways of old? Should you not choose the son who can lead like you?" Esevia's eyes sparked with a subtle defiance.

"The first son... is most like the father." Sharadin replied, his words laboured, revealing the respect he held for tradition.

"That is what the tradition and men of old say. What if they are wrong?" Esevia pressed on, reluctant to move from her position.

"They are not... Esevia, do not attempt to breathe life into this. Folger is a beautiful boy. He carries the head of fire, same as I and our fathers before..." A belch escaped from him before he continued, "But..." a sudden hesitation from him. "Unfortunately, the gods robbed the boy of some wit."

"Do not speak those words... let other people whisper of such things. But not his father." Her sensitivity toward Folger's slowness was etched on her face.

"It is true," honesty beginning to surface with wine's aid. "The boy does not possess a mind for statecraft." Sharadin's bluntness made his annoyance clear.

Esevia's gaze remained steadfast, even in the face of his blunt words. The honesty that surfaced with the aid of wine brought a touch of vulnerability to the room. The flickering flames in the candelabra cast a warm glow, highlighting the contours of the grand chamber and the subtle nuances of the queen's expression. Esevia slowly descended into a reclined pose on her side. Tonare's words flitted through her mind, leaving behind only a fleeting impression.

Breaking eye contact, Sharadin's gaze shifted away from the cerulean windows that mirrored a maternal defensive vexation. There was an unspoken complexity lingering behind those eyes, layers of emotions and thoughts intertwined in the deep recesses of Esevia's gaze. He couldn't quite decipher the intricacies, a reminder that despite the years of shared history, some aspects of his wife's inner world remained elusive. Sharadin made his way to the other side of the bed. The gravity of unspoken words settled between them. He eased himself onto the bed with a sigh.

Esevia grappled with a notion: *perhaps it is not about tradition at all,* she wondered. *Tradition,* she mused. The queen decided to turn her mind away from the topic of succession. Yet, it was merely a temporary diversion, a calculated pause before the inevitable return.

Breaking the pregnant hush, Sharadin heard a surprising question escape from Esevia's side of the bed.

"You will not enter me this night, will you?"

3

Sharadin was quite taken aback by those words. Here, ready to pounce, was another topic he wasn't ready for. Even if he was in a sober state. Again, though, he sensed there was more to what appeared on the surface. He was curious why the drastic shift in conversation. He couldn't shake the feeling that some emotional puppetry was being attempted. Glancing over his shoulder, he saw Esevia's back.

The king cleared his throat before he said, "I have consumed too much wine to be an adequate lover this night."

"Do you utter the same words to whores when you have had countless cups?" a sharp reply from the queen.

Laughter escaped from Sharadin before he could stifle it. "Forgive me, but..." His laughter turned into coughs. Overcoming it, he continued, "If I am not mistaken, you are a queen, not a whore."

He felt the movement in the bed as she turned to face him. "There are times when a queen must be a whore... I would be a whore for you."

The cylinders of thought rolled again; he wondered how the conversation had shifted from succession to intimacy. Of course, Esevia had expressed a displeasure with a certain aspect of their intimacy before. Sharadin had promised to try to improve it. Although he had probably made a promise, he couldn't keep. He knew she was right. Whether sober or drunk, Sharadin has never refused a concubine... after Tirani's death.

"You may prove your skills as a whore... another night," Sharadin said conclusively, his back still facing her.

As he attempted to let the bed envelop him and embrace sweet sleep, a force stopped him. Sharadin, feeling a gentle but insistent tugging, looked over his shoulder to see Esevia staring at him with a handful of his garment clenched in her hands. "No, this night," she said firmly.

"Have you gone shitwitty? Are you that eager to prove your whoredom?" Sharadin questioned, his agitation firmly on the surface. He now turned around to present his face.

"Yes!" Esevia's words remained firm. "That must be the only way to lure you between my thighs. And maybe I will grow used to being loved that way."

"Your words reek of horse's shit; you have received good loving. We have three children–"

"A cold humping... formal and to the point."

Sharadin's features remained mostly stoic, but the widening of his eyes bespoke his surprise. He had been naïve or thought her a fool. How could she not notice his absences of passion and emotion in their intimacy? Sharadin turned away; he refused to maintain the eye lock. He had no rebuttal for her remark. The love he had for Tirani – is not something he believed he could replicate. In the early stages of their union, formality prevailed; the first time he took her to his bed, more an act of necessity rather than desire. This kind of intimacy had consumed the early years of their marriage, with children being the desired outcome. Overtime Sharadin noticed how Esevia's demeanour transformed. Once inexpressive, she began to fervently thrust her hips in those intimate moments. Sharadin would observe the longing in her eyes. He knew she was growing to love him; in a way, he could never return. The king understood her feelings, or he at least believed he did. But between perplexing scrolls and not seeing eye to eye with the most favoured son, Esevia had undoubtedly picked the wrong moment to express these feelings. *Although...* the red-headed king was a man hardened by conquest, politics and generalship. Men like those rarely invite tender conversations – and if they did, perhaps only one woman would ever hear it.

A voice at his back, "Have you no more words for me?"

He felt the slow release of his fabrics that were once clumped in Esevia's hands. Sharadin thought about a reply, then decided against it. The wine was making him consider brutal words. In truth, a good percentage of that was just him. The queen changed position in the bed, as to get a sight of his face. Sharadin sat on the edge, staring, but not really seeing the details.

"Tradition is not the issue, is it?" Esevia spoke in a somewhat accusatory tone. "Nor have my thighs offered you any disrespect." She was glaring at the side of his face. Even in her current state, a part of her was admiring him. Esevia concluded, "It is about Tirani."

"You do not know what you speak of," Sharadin said, his words light.

Esevia, sensing the lack of conviction in his reply, pressed on. "If she had birthed you a second son... and asked for consideration. Would you dismiss her so easily?"

"Yes..." conviction returned.

"I do not believe you."

"Believe what you will!" The king's voice rose. Esevia shuddered a little. "You wish only to spite your sister. What you ask is not for the good of the realm." He turned to her, peering into her face while leaning forward. He added, "The thought of her children on the throne, drive you to madness."

Sharadin wanted to add further words, but he understood he would be stepping into her realm. That's what she wants, for him to indulge in the feelings aspect of this conversation. He wanted to tell her that sex with whores was easier. It felt like an afternoon activity, comparable to hunting or horse-riding. The act was... what was the phrase she used? *A cold humping,* Sharadin thought. Esevia, with all her enticement and allure, the sensuality of her, reminded him of Tirani. The current queen probably possessed more, but he wasn't ready to admit that – not to himself, not to her.

Esevia felt the need to press further. She gained more confidence to speak once Sharadin turned his eyes from her. "If Folger was spawned from Tirani's thighs, would you disregard him so easily?"

Ignoring her inquiry, Sharadin persisted in his attempt to escape the conversation through repose. However, Esevia, fuelled by determination and vulnerability, physically stopped him. Her touch was both a plea and a demand. "You deny me truest affection and harbour them for a ghost," she declared. Her words seem to permeate the dimly lit room. There, in the delicate interplay between light and shadow, the profile of their relationship laid bare.

The candles flickered, casting wavering shadows on the walls. Sharadin, visibly irritated, jaw clenched, continued to ignore her, determined to find solace in the refuge of sleep. The tension between them thickened.

Esevia realised he was on the edge. Determined not to let him escape into the realm of dreams, she said, "You will not sleep until I am answered. Do you prefer cold skin to warm flesh? Is that what gives cock encouragement?"

His jaw clenched even tighter.

The air in the room seemed to constrict.

In a sudden eruption of emotion, Sharadin's composure shattered. Glass surrendering to a force. In an astonishing display of agility for a man of his stature, he moved with an unexpected swiftness. He lunged forward, catching Esevia off guard. Before she could flinch, Sharadin was on top of her. His eyes, usually calm and measured, were now ablaze with intensity. Esevia, pinned beneath him, felt the heaviness of his emotions pressing down. Her legs parted. His hand around her neck.

"You maybe Kozin's daughter, but I swear to Byra, Yius, Sanoma... I will take the breath from you this night, if you refuse to hold tongue," Sharadin's whispered words were almost tangible.

Esevia laid sprawled, eclipsed by the sheer breadth of her husband. Looking up at a face teeming with a mix of anger and frustration. Cascades of red hair framed his features, resembling the branches of a willow tree. Esevia was somewhat frightened and yet aroused. She didn't move a muscle until Sharadin sought to remove his presence from atop her. She wrapped her legs around him in response. While on the surface, she seemed to crave intimacy, hidden beneath the layers in the recesses that Sharadin couldn't penetrate. Esevia was thinking *Tonare was right.*

The door to the royal chamber opened a little, then shut. But the royal couple barely heard it.

COLLECTING WHISPERS

284 BM

1

Ophelia pressed herself against the heavy doors of the grand chamber. She pressed herself against it so tightly that she felt as if she might meld with the door or find herself on the other side. Her ear straining to catch the muffled sounds emanating from within. The act she was committing did not solely fuel the anxiety that gripped. The imminent threat of being discovered by the patrolling guards equally kindled it. In the dimly lit corridor, their steps were a constant reminder of the limited time she had before they would round the corner again. She glimpsed at the jug of wine she had laid on the floor next to her. A part of her wondered why she was taking part in this risky gambit; had her desire and curiosity for freedom always been this present? Did Tonare draw her attention to it, or did he plant the seed? The thick doors occasionally seeped fragments of conversation, some discernible words, others muffled. Ophelia strained to comprehend the discussions within her heart racing. The words that reached her ears were forming a picture - a picture that someone of her standing shouldn't see.

Slowly, her concentration for deciphering the sound crumbled. The distant steps of the guards grew louder. They were coming. Ophelia opened the grand chamber door just enough. She swiftly knelt to retrieve the jug of wine strategically placed on the floor. Cradling the jug close to her body, she waited, heart pounding. The nonchalance she held steady on her face resulted from practice. As the guards turned the corner, Ophelia closed the door with a carefully controlled thud. She then briskly walked past the patrolling figures. Head down.

"Autokrator has had enough of wine," she said, as she passed them like a gentle breeze.

It seemed innocent enough... *But*. Guard one, caught in the quiet of their march, found his mind swirling with a nagging thought - a thought that was a single droplet clinging to a leaf.

Guard one turned to his comrade. "Autokrator sent for more wine... even in the condition we saw him in?" Silence was among them as they continued to march. Guard one looked over his shoulder, eyes narrowing as he observed Ophelia. His inquiry returned. "Did we not see her outside the study room earlier?"

"I believe so. But whatever the room, Autokrator is partial to wine," Guard two responded with a casual dismissal.

Guard one's features were pensive; his suspicion teetered on the edge of earnest inquiry and the whims of paranoia.

"You give too much thought to this," Guard two said from a pragmatic view. "He likely sent for more wine to conclude his evening. His drinking is remarkable, but he may have realised that even he has limits."

Guard one's droplet of suspicion slowly slid from the leaf.

2

Ophelia, a seemingly inconspicuous servant in the grand palace of Bacrea, had long navigated the shadows, her presence barely acknowledged by the courtly denizens. However, a transformative promise hung in the air, whispered to her by Tonare, a promise of freedom that appeared to be the driving force behind her actions. But it wasn't solely the allure of liberation that propelled Ophelia into the heart of courtly intrigue; it was the seductive notion of power – power over her own destiny.

Born in a turbulent time, Ophelia's early years unfolded against the backdrop of political upheaval in Copia. Her family, native to Gelare, migrated to Copia but faced economic hardship because of the Fourth War of the Successors. As the dark clouds of uncertainty gathered, her parents, faced with the harsh realities of displacement and scarcity, made a heart-wrenching decision. Ophelia, at the tender age of eight years, became a casualty of necessity as her parents, grappling with the grim choices that political instability imposed, gave her into servitude. Tonare's words, *not just free but hold position and purpose*, were the true catalyst. They sparked something beneath those shy eyes.

Over the following weeks, the reserved servant with long dark hair moved amongst the court, her presence unfelt and neglected, as she collected whispers. Under the soft glow of countless candles, the grand banquet hall shimmered. As court members gathered for a formal feast, Ophelia discreetly moved among them, carrying trays filled with goblets of wine and plates of numerous delicacies. The air was thick with the aroma of roasted meats and the reverberating melodies of minstrels. Ophelia's ears, however, were perked. They attempted to absorb the sotto voce conversations that took place at the edges of the festivities. Court members, donned in fine garments, shared their opinions on any potential pretenders to the throne. Ophelia, feigning an interest in her duties, lingered near clusters of nobles engaged in animated discussions. Snippets of conversations revealed their preferences and prejudices, painting a vivid picture of court dynamics.

Her next venture led her to the lush embrace of the palace gardens, where she tended to vibrant blooms in the royal sanctuary. Disguised as a diligent servant absorbed in horticultural duties, she overheard courtiers beneath the trees. Their clandestine discussions illuminated Queen Esevia's apparent disdain for Nulynia and her children. As she delicately pruned blossoms, Ophelia, hidden by the idyllic beauty of the garden, extracted morsels of truth from gossipy exchanges that painted intricate portraits of the royal family's relationships.

The bustling marketplace, a lively theatre of commerce and camaraderie, became Ophelia's next arena. Clad in plain servant garb, she navigated through stalls where artisans peddled wares and traders hawked goods. Amid the crowd's hustle and bustle, she exchanged pleasantries with other servants, all the while keenly listening to the conversations of the townsfolk. Rumours about Paterocles' rising favour and Queen Esevia's harboured jealousy murmured through the marketplace like a subtle breeze. Ophelia, skilful in interception, gained insights into the sentiments that simmered among the commoners, revealing that the palace walls did not entirely shield the royal family from the whispers of the people.

Within the heart of the palace, the Council Chamber witnessed weighty discussions shaping the realm's destiny. Entrusted with delivering missives, Ophelia discreetly lingered near the entrance during official meetings. Advisors and courtiers openly praised Tanitos as the king's most reliable confidant, and as she balanced a tray laden with parchments, Ophelia gleaned insights into the political dynamics that unfolded within the council. The voices of those unaware of her presence painted Tanitos as the beacon of wisdom, a figure commanding respect and trust among the elite.

She collected these particles of information, information not just concerning Queen Esevia but other court members as well. Tonare had conveyed his desire for knowledge of the queen's activities specifically. But Ophelia was thinking *information itself* was the real value here. She had no idea of how he would use any information she gave him, but the underhanded way he approached her made Ophelia consider ill intent.

On a day that moved sluggishly, almost as if the day itself carried out duties of a servant, Ophelia would come across another piece of information that only a slave like her would realise, given the slightly special treatment she received from Queen Esevia. Ophelia dragged herself through her duties; there was nothing interesting to overhear on a day like this. She had heard many things already; that was surely useful enough. The monotony of the day had her partake in escapism, as she carried out various tasks, her mind envision herself as someone with position and purpose. Ophelia didn't desire power over anyone. It was autonomy she craved. Being a child that was put into servitude by her parents meant that at no point in her life so far, had she exercised the freedom of choice.

Daydreams continued to envelop her as she carried out her business. The palace embraced a quiet atmosphere as Ophelia approached the Royal Study room. Her eyes found another servant already at work, focused, organising scrolls by their coloured seals. With a subtle nod of acknowledgement, she silently withdrew. As she pivoted away from the study, the dull echo of her footsteps accompanied her journey through the marble corridors. The tedious rhythm of servitude dictating her existence within the grand palace. Arriving at the entrance of the Council Chamber, Ophelia set to work, the monotony of her tasks eclipsed only by the grandeur of the room itself. The heavy wooden furniture that plagued the elongate room conveyed the seriousness that occurred within. As if the wood held onto the spectre of those conversations. Just as she was about to start, the door of the Council Chamber eased open.

3

Paterocles found himself in the grand palace. He couldn't think of another time when he didn't want to be here this much. Nulynia always told him about his inability to present a necessary facade. He hoped the anxiousness below the surface wasn't telling on his exterior. The prince's strides were the opposite of languid, the gaze on his face focused. He was oozing the vibe of a man with a destination to reach. What culminated this was the quick polite nods, that was the extent of his interaction with courtiers who sought a moment of his time. Their attempts to spark conversation were quickly extinguished by the brevity of his replies.

In his possession, carefully concealed, was the source of his unease. The burden nestled discreetly within his attire. Although, Paterocles felt like everyone knew it was there. The palace surroundings blurred in his peripheral vision as he navigated its corridors. At last, he stood before the imposing doors of the Council Chamber. He extended his arm to open them, and there escaped an *errrr*. Paterocles appeared from behind the strained noise, hoping the room was empty, but he found Ophelia.

Paterocles momentarily froze, as if caught in a clandestine act. Hesitation, a ripple across still waters, flittered across the prince's countenance. A subtle shock, until he fully registered the figure of Ophelia, the servant garbed in faded linen. Paterocles' intended solitude interrupted. Attuned to the subtleties of her surroundings, the servant girl perceived the dance of uncertainty that ran across the prince's face.

Her meek nod, a customary acknowledgement, was offered in response to the prince's presence. "Excelletem," she uttered in a soft, deferential tone.

Paterocles, while not getting his initial desire to be alone, felt a sense of relief that only a servant shared the space. One servant, which was better than a group of them being present. He closed the imposing doors behind him, confident that the servant girl wouldn't cause hindrance to his covert activity. His nod, a silent acknowledgement, was directed at Ophelia before he ventured further into the Council Chamber.

She watched the regal fabrics that clothed him with curiosity. What she had perceived was an obvious hesitation from him, but *why*? Ophelia was close to being taken away by a flood of intrigue... but she caught herself.

Paterocles advanced deeper into the room, his footsteps echoing faintly, his gaze sweeping the notable long table that stretched across the centre. Intricate grain patterns nearly melded seamlessly with its rich colour. He proceeded, discerning eyes scanning, seeking the item he required. The desk and writing table were the first area to experience the prince's hunt. Internally, Paterocles lamented the fact that he couldn't undertake this task in the solitude of his estate outside the city, but the wear and tear of time had rendered that option obsolete. Perhaps he should have just come to the palace without the source of his anxiety... But the thought of leaving the letter unattended was more unsettling.

Realising the need for caution, Paterocles contemplated the presence of Ophelia in the room. He would have forgotten her existence completely if not for his state of hypervigilance. Concern crept into his thoughts about her level of attention and whether she might scrutinise his actions.

A moment of pause descended upon Paterocles as he tried to recall the name he had overheard at the forest ritual. "Oh... Ophelia, is it?" he uttered; his tone carried uncertainty.

"That is correct, Excelletem," Ophelia's meek voice murmured. Her attention devoted to polishing and arranging items, the soft swish of a cloth against surfaces accompanied her words.

Paterocles took this moment to engage in conversation. "I must praise your devotion; surrendering your chaste to Byra takes courage." A veneer of courtesy covered his words with a tone that sought to convey both acknowledgement and a subtle attempt to steer attention away from his current mission. He continued his exploration of the desk and writing table, maintaining a facade of casual curiosity, all the while his mind remained tethered to the delicate nature of his concealed intentions.

"Tell me, Ophelia," Paterocles inquired. "What was it like to partake in the forest rites? I know you have witnessed it before, but to be at the centre of it must be a unique experience."

Ophelia responded with measured words while still absorbed in her tasks. "It was Excelletem. I was honoured to be afforded such opportunity... although... nerves held me from start to end."

"Understandable," Paterocles chimed in.

"I think... I feel Byra was honoured with the purity I offered." Ophelia took a moment before she concluded, "I feel closer to her."

Paterocles, though engrossed in his search, kept the conversation flowing. "Yes... there are people that will call upon her for many years and still not know the closeness you speak of." Paterocles was growing frustrated, the item he sought wasn't in the storage compartments of the desk and not present on the surface of the writing table. It was time he moved on. Before he did, he posed another question to Ophelia. "Do you think you will bear a child of Byra? The High Priestess herself is a child of Byra."

Ophelia, absorbed in her task, paused at Paterocles' question. Her expression became manipulated by concern at the unexpected inquiry. The mention of bearing a child caught her off guard, a possibility she hadn't considered before. The weight of such a possibility loomed over her. However, as her thoughts raced, a certain detail emerged in her mind and softened her expression slowly.

She responded, her voice quiet but composed, "No, I believe Excelletem withdrew see–" She halted abruptly, realising the gravity of what she was about to reveal, but in truth she had already said too much. "Grant me pardons," she murmured, her voice barely above a whisper, her eyes downcast in embarrassment. A touch of fright in her demeanour.

Paterocles spoke, sensing her discomfort. "It is no concern. Anyone can have a slip of the tongue." He attempted to ease the tension that lingered. As he made his way over to the cabinets, Paterocles' mind wandered, contemplating the information he had just become privy to. Although it's not something he should know, he couldn't erase it from his mind. Did Tonare's quiet whisper to the king play a role in Ophelia's nomination? And why had he found her in the forest, out of all the other women? *Maybe he sought after her. Could the prince's heart be longing for a servant?* Paterocles thought.

As intriguing as this speculation was, and speculation was all it was, he wasn't aware of Tonare's actual intentions. Paterocles refocused on the reason he was in the Council Chamber. He began to rummage through the cabinets, remembering to add some indifference to his demeanour. A desperate-looking search would probably be a more memorable part of Ophelia's day. He was slightly desperate though, desperate to add the seal to the letter and be rid of it, instead of harbouring it in his possession – especially in the palace. Paterocles' fingers brushed against the smooth surface of a small box, tucked away in a corner. He was touched by anticipation and relief immediately, as he was confident of what the box contained. With careful hands, he retrieved the seal from the box, along with the sealing wax and melting spoon from their resting places within the cabinet.

Meanwhile, Ophelia was engrossed in her duties, though a slight itch of curiosity niggled at her mind. She observed Paterocles with guarded interest from the corner of her eyes. Noting the tension that seemed to thaw out of him as he located certain items.

Paterocles seated himself at the head of the table. His figure failed to occupy the grand chair completely. He placed the seal, wax, and the spoon on the table's surface.

His gaze darted to Ophelia briefly before returning to the wax... She was now preparing to polish the long table with a cloth in hand. Paterocles contemplated his next actions, hesitating momentarily, but as he regarded her, he drifted into his thoughts. While thinking about the letter concealed within his fabrics, the rational part of his mind kicked in. *A mere servant would not possess the ability to read*, Paterocles thought. Realising that the real issue here would be his state of mind and his behaviour, these things might spark an interest in his actions. With this newfound awareness, Paterocles retrieved the letter from his clothing. He held it aloft for a moment, the parchment surface crinkling softly beneath his touch. He examined it while reminding himself that it was not something Ophelia could comprehend. With this confidence, he placed it gently on the table before him, a distinct lack of anxiety in his movements now. He was certain that even if she entered his vicinity (which was likely as she was set to polish the table), she couldn't read the letter even if she caught a glimpse. The prince was no longer concerned about proximity... *But had he miscalculated*?

As the prince melted the wax with a nearby candle flame, Ophelia was now at the head of the table. She proceeded with her cleaning, gazing into the patterns that graced the surface. She was careful not to obstruct his actions. Her eyes occasionally glancing in his direction as she worked. Paterocles poured the wax from the spoon. A pool of wax formed upon the parchment, and he glanced at Ophelia before pressing the seal into it. In that moment, he noticed her eyes taking their time to return to the table, instead they lingered on the parchment.

The beginning of the letter, written in Patin, reads:

Respects at your door, Autokrator Ellisar
I see you have ignored
My initial request for diplomacy
Is this an outright refusal?

Ophelia removed her gaze.

"Just making peace with the nobles," he remarked casually. "They can be an irritating bunch."

There was something the prince wasn't aware of, Ophelia... wasn't like the other servants of the palace. Unlike them, she was personally purchased by Queen Esevia herself. The servant girl's chaste being one reason for her acquisition, along with her unassuming nature, which gave birth to her propensity to be unobtrusive. A quality that probably served strategic politicking purposes... especially when said individual has been secretly taught how to read. The prince's passing remark about the nobles would have been inconsequential, if Ophelia hadn't read the first few lines of the letter. His attempt to make her believe he was writing to the nobles sparked her interest. She now knew he was writing to Ellisar and his efforts to diverge only made it clear that he did not have his father's blessings to do so.

4

Tonare stood in the middle of a room, where the incongruence was loudly evident. The room shrouded in simplicity, not befitting the regality that stood in the middle. Ermis, the Doulos of the palace, had been surprised by Tonare's request to come here. He found it odd that a man of such stature would willingly allow himself to be surrounded by such substandard quality. The atmosphere was still, punctuated only by the faint whisper of fabric and the distant murmurings of the palace beyond. His eyes swept across the room, the small space sparsely furnished, the modesty of the bed so potent he couldn't bear to look at it. Tonare could feel the discomfort anytime his eyes lingered too long. As he floated around the room, his mind wandered, curious about the inhabitant of this humble abode.

Moments had passed since Ermis had led him here, and as Tonare curiously surveyed the room, his eyes settled upon a small storage chest. Without hesitation, he approached the corner it was nestled in. Had he always been such a curious person or was this a special case... His fingers brushed over the worn wood. The weathered surface of the lid lifted. Tonare's eyes and hands began sifting through Ophelia's belongings. He wasn't after a particular item, nor did he intend to pry, although his actions were no doubt invasive. Led by his curiosity, he sought to get more of an understanding of Ophelia's character. It wasn't until his fingers brushed against the soft fabric of her undergarments, a flush of heat rising to his cheeks, that he thought he'd done enough. But as he pushed her delicates to the side, the tips of his fingers rubbed against the bottom of the chest. With an investigative touch, he detected a discrepancy in the alignment, a subtle irregularity. He pressed down on the panel. The false bottom lifted, revealing a cache of parchment. Curiosity was about to flood, but Tonare heard a cough growing towards the door. He just managed to return the chest to its original state and stand up in time.

Ophelia's hand pushed the door open, revealing Tonare's unexpected presence. Her eyes widened in surprise. For a moment she stood frozen in the doorway, her heart had jumped slightly in her chest.

"Excelletem, what brings you to my quarters?" she enquired as she stepped into the room, still trying to shake off the surprise that coursed through her veins. Tonare's explanation centred around their discussion during the forest rites. Ophelia expected they would meet again, but perhaps not like this. She walked past him, visibly tense, and as she sat down, her eyes were filled with contemplation.

"You wish to go back on our agreement?" Tonare spoke in an unusually gruff tone. His voice clearly revealed his disappointment. Ophelia remained silent for a few moments, and Tonare wasn't surprised. He could tell by the way she traipsed into the room that this would be the nature of their interaction.

"I wish not to go back, but forward," a small voice pierced the silence and ceased Tonare from making his way to the door.

"Then why do you hold tongue?"

"I am a slave, but not a fool," Ophelia replied, a trace of assertion in her voice.

Tonare's eyes held a brief flash of surprise as they fell on the dainty figure that sank onto the surface of the bed. Her long dark hair trailing to the small of her back; it reminded him of his mother's.

Ophelia regarded Tonare with a guarded expression from the corner of her eyes. She continued, "Position and purpose, those were your words. I would see you give meaning to them before my tongue can come loose."

Tonare paused to survey the unpretentious room, its rough-hewn stone walls enclosing the space with an air of humble austerity. As he settled onto the bed, his movements betrayed a subtle aversion, a reluctance echoed in the slight hesitation before he finally seated himself. He had scrutinised the modest bed in his mind, and though he begrudgingly relented to sit, it was more out of necessity than comfort. Tonare's thoughts churned inside his mental universe as he pondered Ophelia's demand for clarification. The words position and purpose echoed in his mind. He struggled to conceive an explanation that would resonate with her, his understanding limited by his unfamiliarity with her personal story. He had come seeking information, hoping to glean insights that could aid him in his own ambitions, but he found himself attempting to philosophise. While he wasn't aware of her personal story, he understood the inherent limitations of her station as a slave.

In his eyes, her purpose was not one of her own choosing, but rather a role imposed upon her by the whims of fate. "Would you not like to choose a purpose for yourself?" he finally ventured. "To feel as though life is something that you have a hand in shaping, rather than something that is simply happening to you? Would you not like a position that brings you pride? I can see you being nobility." Tonare was seated on the narrow end of the bed. Facing forward, Ophelia sat along the length of the bed, her back turned towards him. A silence washed over the room, pronouncing Ophelia's scepticism.

"Nobility... how would I attain that?" she spoke after a drawn-out pause, a slight titter in her voice.

"Land and coin," Tonare replied, taking no time to consider the question.

The prince was about to form words, perhaps to further elaborate on achieving noble status, but Ophelia's words cut his own. "Marriage..." She spoke. "I feel that would be better."

"... I think you correct," Tonare said with some surprise in his tone. Probably impressed that she thought of that. "Yes, attaching yourself to a noble name that has history may prove to be a better path than building one from the ground." He stood up and turn to face her. Her back instead of the youthful plump of her face greeted him. "Once your freedom is acquired, the nobleman you wish to form union with must be pious. The absence of your chaste due to the forest rites is something he would be understanding of."

She turned in his direction. Her brown eyes looked up at him.

He continued, "Have I given meaning to my words and–"

"I believe you have misunderstood, Excelletem."

There was puzzlement on Tonare's face.

"I do not seek marriage to a nobleman... the marriage I speak of... is with you." Ophelia asserted.

The confusion that once plagued Tonare's face faded into amusement. He found the proposition outrageous. All that could escape his lips were, "Shitwitty."

"I have not lost wit," Ophelia defended.

"Perhaps you are in the process of losing it," Tonare replied.

In Ophelia's quarters, the dim light gave birth to shadows that danced against the stone walls. The faint scent of incense present in the air. The exchange between the Ahdian prince and the unassuming servant unfolded. Tonare's face held a scornful expression. The wavering light illuminated the delicate features of Ophelia's face as she awaited Tonare's response.

"I must say, the temerity you possess is unbecoming for a slave," Tonare scoffed, his voice filled with haughtiness, his gesture a sharply pointed finger. "To suggest that a prince of Ahdia should take a former slave as his wife is beyond absurd. The scandal would stain the royal indigo."

Ophelia's dark brown eyes met his gaze squarely, the prince's derision not enough to deter her. "Perhaps, but only a king can elevate a woman to the status of queen," she countered, her voice calm but firm. "Regardless of race, creed, tongue. If a king says a woman is a queen, then a queen she is. The people and the court will say Autokratia in her presence." Although she defended her position well, there was a twinge deep inside. She understood that the prince's attitude was because of her position, but she still felt undesirable.

Tonare fiddle with his gold bracers as he wandered aimlessly until he leaned against the hewn stone wall. Hesitation plagued his aristocratic features, something Ophelia was paying acute attention to. He stood, considering her demand, but he didn't fully convince himself.

The servant girl gave him a nudge...

"Remember our conversation in the forest, Excelletem?" Ophelia asked as she stood, then tracing the edge of the bed before sitting again. Her tone tinged with a hint of threat. "I am sure the king and queen would be intrigued by what you asked of me."

Tonare's brow furrowed in confusion. "You would have to break the sanctity of the ritual in order–"

"The taboo you speak of is in regard to details of intercourse. The words we exchanged are not covered by any sanctity," Ophelia interrupted, her voice steady despite the tremor of fear beneath the surface. "I could reveal what we spoke of. The request for me to spy on Queen Esevia."

Tonare's eyes widened in alarm, "Is that so..." He spoke in a low tone, as he grew even more surprised by Ophelia's boldness. It would seem the delicate daffodil had some thorns he was unaware of.

"Agree to my terms," Ophelia declared, "Then neither one of us will have to tread that path." Tonare continued to stare, trying to figure out the cause for the boldness she was displaying. Under the exterior, however, Ophelia's heart thumped hard. If the prince was aware of the anxiousness, and the uncertainty that swelled within her... He would have laughed at her proposal. But he wasn't aware. Tonare, once leaning against the wall lost in thought, now stood upright, prepared to comply with Ophelia's demand, albeit reluctantly. However, there was one more thing the slave needed.

"I mean no offence, Excelletem," she spoke softly, hesitation apparent in her voice. Her eyes darted nervously, exposing the anxiousness that threatened to boil over. "But your word alone will not do. I need an oath to Byra, and a vow of death if agreement is broken."

The request lingered in the air. As Tonare gazed at Ophelia, he expected to feel a surge of anger at her audacious demands. After all, she was attempting blackmail, and her request for an oath of death was not something to be taken lightly. Yet, to his surprise, anger was not the predominant emotion coursing through him. Instead, he found himself intrigued by Ophelia's boldness. A dark part of him looked on with admiration. He felt strangely captivated. In that moment, her unkempt hair and humble attire seemed to fade into insignificance, revealing a beauty that rivalled even the most regal of women. Tonare took the oath.

"Very well, I shall reveal to you the things I have learnt from collecting whispers," Ophelia said, her voice low. She went over to the small chest and retrieved a brush. She sat back on the bed and continued, "Queen Esevia holds a bitter heart towards Nulynia and her children. Maybe they never agreed with each other even in their early years, but that is something you would know... Paterocles has gained more favour with the common people, something that pushes the queen to madness. Even if the king would break tradition and consider another heir, rebellion would probably occur if the people do not see Paterocles on the throne. This the queen knows, and yet her desire for Folger to succeed remains. However, one might wonder about this passionate push for Folger... Who truly holds the reins of power?" Ophelia brushed her hair gently, restoring some neatness to it after the day had dishevelled it. "Tanitos is the only true advisor to the king," she continued. "Anyone who has witnessed the political counsel of this realm knows that the other advisors hold title but are not truly heard."

Tonare listened intently, though he remained outwardly composed. Inwardly, the cogs of his mind turned. Contemplating how best to use this newfound knowledge to his advantage.

"I suspect your goal must be similar to the queen's... power, the throne," she said, pausing her brushing and turning her attention to his face. His features made it clear he was physically present but not mentality. "I say this to cut a straight path," Ophelia added. "To the information, you will find more intriguing."

This jolted Tonare, allowing him to escape the walls of his inner workings. The way she spoke gave life to his fascination. Lines of curiosity formed on his brow; he took a step forward with bated breath.

"Paterocles is contacting Ellisar without Sharadin's blessing," she revealed.

Tonare's eyes widened in astonishment.

"Why would –," he stopped himself from completing the question, knowing *why* Paterocles would do it. The real *why* was why take such a risk? "How are you aware of this?" Tonare asked. He didn't know whether he truly doubted her, but questions were threatening to flood.

"Their differences on the matter of war, that is the likely fuel."

"How are you aware of this!?" Tonare demanded.

"I listen and I see. But no one sees me."

LAVACRUM

284 BM

.

1

Tonare wandered the corridors of the palace. The hour was late. His thin linen gown, a hue of light blue, billowed as he strolled. The memory of the slip of parchment lingered in his mind. He thought about the message written upon it. He could no longer refer to the bit of material, as he had reduced it to ash. The mental imagery of it was all he had. Tonare recalled the evening it had been surreptitiously delivered to him. In the bustling atmosphere of the evening meal, Tonare sat amidst the throng, his thoughts consumed by matters of politics and power. The aromas of meat and spices filled the banquet hall; firelight and oil lamps cast a warm amber glow, warding off the darkness. As present minds were enthralled by the revelry, Queen Esevia discreetly signalled one of her trusted chambermaids, a silent messenger at her fingertips. With a small slip of parchment concealed in her palm, the chambermaid waited for the opportune moment to execute her covert orders. As the servants circulated, replenishing goblets and clearing plates, the chambermaid positioned herself strategically near Tonare's seat. Her movements were subtle, her demeanour reserved yet purposeful. Then the moment presented itself. As Tonare reached for his cup of wine, the chambermaid deftly slipped the parchment under the base of his goblet, ensuring it remained concealed from view. Tonare, engrossed in conversation with nobles, remained oblivious to the covert exchange taking place beneath his very nose. Later, as the banquet drew to a close and guests departed, Tonare lifted his cup to prepare for a final toast. It was then that his fingers brushed against the hidden missive nestled beneath the base of the goblet. His brow furrowed in confusion as he retrieved the parchment, its surface smooth against his fingertips. With a sense of foreboding, he opted not to unfurl the parchment in the presence of others.

Tonare continued to move toward his destination. While he did so, his thoughts drifted once more. This time he reflected on his conversation with Posidius, regarding the piece of parchment that had been so stealthily delivered to him. The memory of their exchange seemed to intrude involuntarily upon his current mind. Posidius' words had that eerie ability. To superimpose themselves upon one's mind, no matter the resistance. In their conversation, Posidius had cautioned him against underestimating Queen Esevia's cunning, emphasising the dangers of feeling too confident in his ability to manipulate her to achieve his ambitions. Although Posidius' cautious nature threatened to exasperate, Tonare knew it was his job to be a constant reminder of the treacherous waters he navigated in pursuit of power.

The prince finally arrived at his purpose. He was greeted by the sight of the arched entrance, standing tall and imposing, reaching nearly nine feet in height. The archivolt framing the entrance was adorned with motifs of grapes and vines curving gracefully, their leaves and tendrils intricately detailed in the cool cream marble. As Tonare proceeded toward the tall reddish-brown door, he noted the tympanum. He regarded the goddess' serene expression, whispering a quiet prayer to himself. Of course, he referred to the goddess as Otia. His palm pressed against the thick door of the Royal Baths, as it yielded Tonare thought about the potential outcome of this furtive meeting with his sister.

2

The entrance to the Royal Baths cracked open, the warm glow of light spilled forth from within. Tonare met the sluice sounds of the bath fountains, its gentle melody constant, a therapeutic chime. In the silence of the night, the sound of flowing water easily filled the space, and yet the volume of it didn't hinder relaxation. In fact, it aided it. Tonare removed the sandals on his feet before venturing further into the bathhouse. A subtle mint fragrance dominated, a refreshing welcome. He thought about how to go about the conversation with his sister. They held little love for each other. This, naturally, made her suspicious and guarded when dealing with him. He didn't need her defensive... scrutinising. He needed her cooperative, overconfident, and misjudging. Tonare made his way toward the marble benches on the outskirts, his bare feet gracing the smooth surface beneath. They grew damper as he stepped. As he sat, his gaze swept over the thin colonnades surrounding the grand bath. The warm waters did not possess the heat to create a steamy atmosphere, just a haze was present for Tonare to look through. *Why here?* Tonare thought, while laying his sandals beside him on the bench. He tried to resist speculating too much. What was important was the meeting itself. He was sure it would be about succession, manoeuvring to ensure one of her children succeed, namely Folger. Also, him getting his desire for military authority, well not his actual desire, just one he needed her to believe.

From a shadowed corner, no, more like a crevice to Tonare's eyes. A figure was escaping the black. *Another Entrance?* Tonare thought, *yes of course this place would hold such secrets*. Slowly, the figure became distinguishable, as the light from the sconces on the wall fell upon her. Despite his surface level dislike, he found her gracefulness admirable. She carried herself in a manner that suggested most things were beneath her. Even him. The light illuminated fair blonde hair, coiled into a bun. With her hair this way, Queen Esevia's features were accentuated, her blue gaze colder.

Tonare patiently observed, Esevia continued to move gracefully beneath the light of the sconces, her naked skin partially covered by a pink mesh gown. The fullness of her pubic garden on display, a bold statement of her unapologetic femininity. She walked with her sandals clutched in her hands, the rhythmic tapping of her footsteps echoing softly against the marble floors. The dampness creating a slight squelch each time. Sitting on a marble bench across from Tonare, the width of the grand bath between them, the prince could still feel the aura she exuded. As if she was in complete control.

He was wondering if she intended to speak from this distance, noting how well the sound of pouring water captured the space; he considered how impractical that would be. Tonare then watched in surprise as Esevia disrobed, the delicate fabric of her gown falling away to reveal the smooth curves of her body. Esevia then eased into the water like a swan, the surface rippling gently in her wake. She continued to glide toward him, her movements fluid and elegant.

Tonare was momentarily taken aback by her sudden approach. As he watched her, he was sure he saw her lips moving. But he heard nothing over the sound of the sluicing water. This prompted him to leave the bench and emerge from the aisle, leaning on a nearby colonnade. "I did not hear your words," he confessed, his voice barely audible over the sound of pouring water.

"Get in," Esevia replied, her voice much louder than before. "I do not wish to shout this night."

Tonare hesitated for a moment, his gaze lingering on Esevia's form as she floated in the water. Despite his reservations, he saw little alternative. So, he removed his garments, the cool marble floor beneath his feet a sharp contrast to the warmth of the water. As he immersed himself in the bath, his eyes lingered on her curiously. Awkwardness clearly written in his body language.

This was clear for the queen to see.

"Resist the tension that plagues you," she said without a blink. "We both know I am not the sister you would fuck, nor you the brother I would part thighs for."

An uneasy smirk was all he could muster in response to her bluntness.

For some reason, a silence grew among them. The offspring of the Koziniac Dynasty looked on at each other while partially immersed in the water. Although she had instigated this rendezvous, admitting Tonare's predictions were correct wasn't something she felt ready to do.

Tonare plucked a conversation from the air. Any conversation.

"I am convinced you are not after my loins," Tonare's words broke the silence. "But meeting here, under the cover of dark. Robes thrown away, flesh-"

"Can you hear that?" Esevia cut through his words.

Tonare was subtly confused. His head swivelled, the ends of his dark blonde hair – now soaked – slightly flashed. He looked around, trying to ascertain what noise Esevia was referring to. But all he could hear was water.

She proceeded, "Did you hear my words before?"

A shake of the head was Tonare's response.

"Any shadows attempting to listen will only hear water," she explained. "Unless they share the same distance as you and I," she said while glancing down at the warm water between them. "They will hear nothing."

It then became clear to Tonare that the location chosen was very intentional. In the back of his mind, he considered Posidius' caution.

"It seems your foresight was correct," Esevia finally admitted.

"How so?" He knew, but wanted her to say it.

"I have lacked the conviction to see my desires come to life," Esevia confessed. *A soft cock*, she whispered so low it was almost inaudible. "I have been lying to myself." Even when she spoke of her flaws, she did so with pride, her chin raised as she looked at Tonare. "I let myself believe words could get me what I want. But the king will not abandon the ways of old," a glint of reproach in her eyes.

Tonare recognised the sincerity in her voice. Somewhat amazed that her words didn't have to battle more reluctance.

"I will not sit by while it unfolds," she affirmed. "While my son is not even given *consideration*." She spoke through gritted teeth as her passion seeped.

As Tonare stood in the basilican bath, his sister's frustrated face and bare chest before him, he wondered about her support for Folger. She was clearly no fool, and yet her belief in Folger deserving consideration was indeed foolish. He cast his mind back on moments where he came across the little imbecile. His head, a mop of tousled red hair, that seemed to be in perpetual disarray. He recalled trying to spark conversation with the boy, only to find no meaningful reply. He formed words filled with awkward pauses and nonsensical tangents. His soft and unassuming features lacking the sharpness of intellect, the wide-set eyes he possessed often unfocused and sometimes appearing vacant. It was clear the boy didn't possess the wit for courtly intrigue, a deficiency the prince was counting on to fulfil his true ambitions. Tonare wasn't aware of this, but there were rumours suggesting the king being a man of many years, impregnated Esevia with tired seed. That was the rational for Folger's predisposition. Of course, no one spoke those words to the king. Tonare was still trying to wrap his mind around it. *She is no fool*; he thought. The cogs were turning, and Tonare mused about the complex nature of maternal love. While the loyalty in the face of the inadequacies was admirable... The illogical devo–

And then *Bing,* illumination. Something Ophelia had said about the reins of power.

He saw past the surface, and beyond that there were other possibilities. Looking at it from another angle, he surmised that Esevia's campaigning for Folger was perhaps a ruse. The person she really wanted with the power of the crown was herself.

Tonare noted Posidius' warning.

3

In the oblong space formed with ceramic and now filled with warm water, the eldest son of the Koziniac Dynasty prepared to discuss covert matters that would grow far more sinister than he had bargained for. He observed how Esevia alternated between treading water and going on the tips of her toes to maintain buoyancy.

"We will need a plan if our desires are going to become flesh," Tonare stated. She looked at him, brows furrowed, probably still feeling the anger from her earlier words. Tonare fed the silence with silence... for a few moments. Under the shining of the sconces, the queen's pale skin appeared porcelain-like. The smoothness of it was prominent as the warm light illuminated it. The queen's lips were now crumpled, hinting at the turmoil of emotions churning within her, like a labyrinth threatening to engulf her. Tonare recognised this and attempted to refocus Esevia's attention back to the practicalities. "Sabotage," he said.

Esevia lifted her gaze from the water and presented puzzled features that asked for clarity.

"His reputation," Tonare explained. "His influence among the commoners is growing vastly. That, along with tradition, strengthens his position greatly. But if we can tarnish this, it may very well create an opportunity for another to be considered for succession."

Esevia's face didn't twitch, considering Tonare's suggestion. He furrowed as her stone features looked at him.

"I am not sure that is the correct path," the queen stated.

"Oh," Tonare responded, his tone showing his questioning of her perspective.

"Reputations can be mended. Scandals and mistakes may be forgiven with time."

Tonare became a little pensive as he listened; trying to predict where this line of thought was headed.

"Tarnishing his reputation will not be enough," Esevia argued. She then made her way to the edge of the bath, tired of treading water. As Tonare watched her, he considered whether he should divulge what Ophelia told him. But he felt conflicted. In his mind, only he and Ophelia were aware of this information... and it was *precious*. What if he was ceding advantage? Although this may be a good way to show her that there is a path for tarnishing reputation. He gently strode through the water, following Esevia's direction. Tonare was concerned about maintaining subtle control over the narrative. Esevia could get carried away with the information and involve him less in the decision-making process. However, as he approached the bath's edge, his pondering made him realise something – that Esevia had the clearest motivation of anyone in the court and acting unilaterally could put her at risk.

With this perspective, he successfully convinced himself that sharing the information may not be to his detriment. Although he didn't have an exact plan laid out, this could be the necessary step to sway her towards the reputation-tarnishing scheme.

"I still believe the reputation path is best," Tonare began the attempted persuasion. "There is a piece of information that could bring you to my reasoning. I will not reveal how I came to possess this knowledge, but you can place confidence in it."

Esevia's eyes seem to assess Tonare with a peculiar intensity, her gaze probing, searching, as if her eyes could physically pry the information from him and how he came to possess it. Tonare felt the force of her scrutiny. Pressing his back against the edge of the bath, his wingspan outstretched. The queen noted the stillness on his face, framed by strands of dark blonde hair.

"The current heir to the Sharad Dynasty," Tonare revealed. "Is in contact with Ellisar... absent the king's approval."

Esevia's reaction was immediate. A flinch of mild shock crossed her features that seemed a little pretentious, quickly replaced by an incredulous expression. Tonare could sense the doubt threatening to spill forth in words, prompting him to reaffirm his statement. "You can place confidence in this," he insisted, his tone firm.

As Tonare awaited her response, he watched intently as Esevia's demeanour shifted. Her initial scepticism slowly taken over by begrudging acceptance, her features softening slightly as she processed the gravity of the revelation.

"Well," she began, her voice tinged with a newfound resolve, "If this holds true, like you say. Then it is indeed something we can use." Tonare observed as a transformation occurred in Escvia's expression. A wide smile, almost unnatural, slowly spreading across her lips. The wide grin revealed her unusually sharp canines, a smile he saw only a few times in his childhood. He resisted the urge to wince at the ominous feeling that accompanied her smile. With that sort of expression, he knew his attempts to convince her of a subtle approach had turned to blood. But perhaps blood was always what she wanted.

The sinister energy that the queen exuded was palpable. Tonare found himself searching for words that would dispel the current feeling in the atmosphere. Esevia moved closer to him, her smile and now her nakedness encouraging his unease.

"With this..." she whispered, excitement brimming. "We can do more than tarnish... we can send him to the plains of the afterlife."

Tonare's non-compliance was clear on his face.

"Why do you object? This path brings our desires more certainty."

Tonare remained still.

"I see," Esevia said as she deciphered his pause. "Nulynia."

The clear waters of the bath embraced him, reaching just below his chest. Tonare could really feel the dark intent, Esevia now in proximity. The heavy energy seeming to ooze from her pores. Tonare had thoughts of objection crowding his throat, yet he swallowed them back, understanding the futility of voicing denial. If Esevia could decipher his silence, his words would surely fare no better under her scrutinising gaze. In this moment, the complexity of his psyche was slowly beginning to unfurl. Jeopardising Paterocles' position as heir, meant to indirectly hurt Nulynia. Although the way he saw it playing out, Paterocles would at least keep his life. The Memories that now played on the screen of his mind were past conversations of Posidius' admonitions. The advisor's voice chastising his tendency towards denial.

Ever since Tonare left the shores of Ahdia, the path he was embarking upon was destined to be filled with tough choices. But he couldn't accept being the eldest son who was robbed of his birthright. To stay in Ahdia and watch his younger brother prance about with all the regal authority he was meant to possess. He wanted to rule *badly*. His ambitions, as sharp and demanding as the cold ceramic under his feet. The death of Paterocles, as expedient as it might seem for his ambitions, would leave scars not easily healed on Nulynia. He continued to search himself inwardly. Surely during all the scheming and cunning, he must have considered Paterocles' elimination. How would he usurp the throne while the rightful heir draws breath? Is there enough tarnishing in the world to allow that? Paterocles' death would mean Folger as an heir, even if reluctantly. The inadequacies of the boy would mean the court and people would long for a different ruler. King Sharadin's first marriage only produced one son, and Esevia's other sons would certainly not be considered for the throne. The water lapped gently at his skin, a mirror to the turmoil within. The compartmentalisation that had served him so well was beginning to show cracks, letting in the harsh light of consequence.

Pap! Esevia's palm aggressively bounced off the water's surface, regaining Tonare's attention. His right eye blinked to stop the droplets. Esevia painted an annoyed figure.

"You approached me claiming you can give aid, only to freeze at opportune moment," Esevia said. Her lips pressed into a thin line.

"I but give strategic thought," Tonare denied. Even he didn't believe his words as they left his lips.

"Shit from a horse's arse. You came all this way, only to present a soft cock in the face of your ambitions. Does she me–"

"And are you so sure of your convictions?" Tonare pushed back. "The woman who tried to whisper words in her husband's ear, knowing they would fail. Can you see this through without a second thought, knowing your husband will lose most favoured son?"

Her momentum was toward him, not having to travel too far, her smooth nakedness pressed against his. He was uncomfortable. Not so much because he could feel her nipples and pubic garden, but the expression on her face. She pushed her face closer to his, Esevia's cold blue eyes pinned. "I have given him three boys he can love," the queen whispered. "I will see Paterocles dead... to give my desires life." Esevia's cold blue stare peered into him, the intensity of her emotions travelling to his soul. Tonare's body threatened to shudder. He searched for something to say, anything that could steer them away from this precipice.

"I urge you to think beyond any blood thirst," he murmured with a weak tonality, as he stepped back to reintroduce some space between them. The words hanging in the space he created, devoid of conviction.

"Blood thirst?" Esevia questioned, unmoved. "I but seek most reliable path." She spoke so matter-of-factly, as if a man's life didn't hang in the balance. "If he lives, then there remains a chance for him to remove whatever blemish you intend to put on him... you need a stronger gut brother."

Tonare winced. He didn't care for her tone. The objection he just delivered, though, sounded hollow. Even to his own ears. What was this part of him that clung to the hope that there was another way? One absent blood and betrayal. Was it solely Nulynia? No. It was his resolve. He was coming face to face with the beast he intended to tame and found himself a statue at the pivotal act. Standing there, the warm water of the bath enveloping him, he couldn't help but question himself. Would subtlety bring him closer to the throne, or was it merely a veil for his hesitance to do what was necessary?

Swallowing his doubts and basically conceding his previous display of weakness, Tonare shifted the conversation. "How do you intend to use the letters to achieve what you speak of?" he asked.

Esevia floated forward, attempting to close the gap between them. Tonare's outstretched arm stopped her. Her lips curved into a sly smile. "Treason," the queen said. Tonare felt a chill that had nothing to do with the water. "That is something I know, the court and the people will not forgive. If we can intercept or falsify a letter to paint Paterocles as a traitor, conspiring with Ellisar... well, there is no coming back from that."

Treason, Tonare thought. *When did she think of that? Not only the idea, but a path to it.* His eyes were downcast at the water, then he lifted them.

He saw the re-emergence of Esevia's grin. Canines sharp.

PLACING
THE
PIECES

284 BM

1

In the months following Esevia's shadowed proposition, Bacrea's royal palace, with its cold stone and whispering corridors, bore silent witness to a conspiracy that promised to shift the very foundation of the Sharad Dynasty. As time unfurled its days like a scroll of fate, Tonare and Esevia found themselves entwined in a plot of such magnitude that each clandestine meeting, each shared glance, carried the weight of impending history. The warmth of summer gave way to the crisp onset of winter, while there were a few days of apricity, they gradually became non-existent. Tonare felt the atmosphere within the palace walls thicken with tension – a transformation perceptible only to those privy to the dark undercurrents attempting to shape the realm's future. The air grew colder, not just with the season's change but with the anticipation of the plot's unfolding. The corridors, once mere pathways to serve both duties and diversions, now seemed to possess an eerie aura. Almost echoing with the gravity of their secret. With each meeting, as autumn leaves fell and winter's powder began to dust the palace grounds, Tonare sensed himself drifting further into the depths of a scheme from which there was no turning back. He wanted Esevia to have the illusion of control, but he was beginning to think she may really have it. Of course, he would never confess this to Posidius. It was in these moments, usually shrouded in night's innate secrecy, that he questioned whether he was truly embracing his ruthlessness or merely cornering it, shoving it into a box to allow denial.

Their meetings, always shrouded in the utmost secrecy, were arranged with equally underhanded moves. They became the forge upon which their plan was hammered into shape. Esevia, revealing her strategic side, outlined each step with a precision that both awed and unsettled Tonare. He considered whether she could be outwitting him. She was the daughter of Kozin Salvator after all. It was in one such gathering, under the guise of night, that she spoke of Tanitos – King Sharadin's voice of reason and calm. His presence a potential thorn in their side, she noted, given his ability to quell the very chaos they hoped to seed. "Tanitos has the king's ear, more than any other," she mused, her voice a low thrum. "He has the ability to bring calm to him, as well as any hostile situation." Her eyes gleamed with a coldness. "But you need not worry. I have plans that will ensure he cannot rob us of the uncertainty in which we desire to give life to."

Tonare recalled Ophelia's insights into the court's dynamics and understood that Esevia's actions may prove vital. Removing Tanitos from the equation was no minor feat; it was a move that would leave King Sharadin without his most trusted advisor at a time when suspicion and paranoia were to be their closest allies. As winter's hold on the land tightened, so too did their focus on the letter. Tonare's primary concern lay with the ink – the strokes, the nuance of handwriting. "We cannot replicate the subtleties of his hand," he voiced one evening, his brows knitted in concern.

"That is why the seal is paramount," Esevia countered with confidence. "The seal will draw the eye, lend authenticity where doubts might otherwise fester. Once Paterocles admits to the correspondence, the nature of his handwriting will become a secondary concern." Her logic was irrefutable; the admission of contact with Ellisar, regardless of its intent, would cast a shadow too long for Paterocles to escape. Tonare questioned why Paterocles would give admission, but the queen was certain that a direct question would be asked. Esevia detailed her plan to gain the seal with a meticulousness that left little room for error. Her usual disinterest in the Council Chamber's politics provided the perfect cover for her unusual directive – a thorough cleaning of the room under the guise of preparing for the new year's council. It would be during this orchestrated distraction that Ophelia would secure the seal, a brief but critical theft that would lend their forgery the approval of royalty. Following her detailed exposition, Esevia paused, her gaze settling on Tonare. "Who?" she mused aloud, calculation in her voice. "Who will pen the letter to create the convincing formality we need?" The question lingered, a silent challenge to their conspiracy's next critical step. Before Tonare could fully ponder possibilities, Esevia offered her solution. "Posidius," she declared, her suggestion seeming to materialise from the darkness of their scheme. Maybe just a dark crevice of her mind.

"Posidius?" Tonare question. "Surely we can perform some puppetry on a scribe."

"Yes, of course we could attempt such," Esevia admitted, her face cradled by her hands. "But the risks are too great."

"Yes," Tonare said, meeting her line of thought. "It is possible that the scribe could be compelled to confess. If not right away, in the near future."

"Precisely," she grinned. "Posidius possesses the mastery in statecraft and the art of diplomatic correspondence. More importantly, he is loyal to you and your ambitions." Her rationale was sharp. In Esevia's mind, and now seeded into Tonare's, Posidius was not just a participant in their plot but its pivotal instrument – a choice that would lend their forgery an air of authenticity.

Believing they had reached a conclusion, Tonare turned his back and missed the brief, macabre smile that flashed across Esevia's face. "There is something else we must consider to ensure success," her voice just above a whisper. Tonare froze. "In an effort to capture the essence of Paterocles in our correspondence," she continued. "Posidius must become acquainted with his manner of speech, his vernacular. It is the subtleties that lend credence to a forgery."

Tonare's brow furrowed. "Are you not giving too much thought to this? If the seal draws the eye as it should, will the wordage be under such scrutiny?"

"Perhaps not," Esevia said, her face beginning to form a displeased expression. "Let us not consider detail and leave our ambitions to fate. Is this the shitwit you wish to display once you wear a crown?"

The prince felt the sarcasm and the mockery. However, it was her tone that he really didn't care for. Sure, he wanted her to have the illusion of control, but in that moment, he felt like a pawn and not a co-conspirator. "Do not mistake me for your boy!" Tonare said, the words flew from his mouth. Then in a calmer manner he continued, "I but pose reasonable question."

Esevia was now nodding after her initial flinch. A smile played on her lips. "Grant me pardons, dear brother." They both knew the statement wasn't heartfelt. "I simply suggest we apply caution where we can. There will be many eyes, one could be filled with such scrutiny."

Doubt was successfully planted in Tonare's mind. He couldn't ignore the possibility. The general admiration for Paterocles could compel a courtier to really look. He stood in silence; the silence conveying his acknowledgement of Esevia's words.

"Casual exchanges could provide invaluable insights." she lifted the silence before returning to a pause. Esevia watched him keenly before continuing. "Consider it a strategic alignment. Posidius' interactions with Paterocles will be nothing out of the ordinary, just a seasoned advisor offering counsel. It is common enough in the courts and will raise no suspicions. But the benefits to our cause will be significant."

Tonare considered her words, the layers of their plot deepening. Esevia's plan was meticulous, leaving little to chance. Yet, was there more going on behind the icy blue marbles that sometimes keenly analysed Tonare. What was this feeling he had? Something was scratching at him, demanding his attention. He nodded slowly, resigned to the necessity of Esevia's strategy. "Very well," he conceded. "I shall speak with Posidius. I will explain the importance of this…"

Esevia's smile broadened. The pieces were falling into place.

2

Weeks went by since the steps of the plan had been finalised. Tonare's reservations slowly melted away, as he grew warmer to the idea of Posidius composing the letter. He approached Posidius, knowing that the trusted advisor's pragmatism was something he could rely on. The necessity of their act was made clear, and Posidius understood the importance of the role he was to play. Over the years, Posidius had evolved from merely an advisor to the cornerstone of Tonare's political edifice, his counsel as crucial to the prince's ambitions as the very air he breathed. A particular memory surfaced, as clear as a brightly lit day, shedding light on the foundation of their relationship. It was a moment of unvarnished truth. Early in Tonare's political foray, Posidius, with his characteristic bluntness, had stated: "In matters of politics and power, there are no good people."

This maxim was to serve as an anchor, a reminder that morality was a luxury seldom afforded to those who played in the game of power. This recollection drove him from Ahdia, along with Posidius, informing him of something he had been naïve to:

his father's intention to leave the crown to Kozin, the younger. Why else was a sceptre made for him?

Tonare knew that Posidius' loyalty was not to the machinations of power for its own sake but to the vision of what Tonare aspired to achieve. In their many discussions, Posidius had often served as the voice of reason, tempering Tonare's impulses with pragmatic advice. Posidius had never wavered, even when the path took them through moral ambiguity and ethical quandaries. He understood that pursuing power necessitated stepping into grey areas where the distinction between right and wrong blurred. It was this understanding that allowed Tonare to lean on Posidius. He needed him, not just for the success of this scheme, but perhaps for life itself.

The advisor found himself in the company of Paterocles on several occasions, each meeting orchestrated with casual finesse that belied its true purpose. Posidius was a master weaver of conversations. The threads his words carried were invisible to the target. They subtly extracted the deepest thoughts of the intended individual. His encounters with Paterocles were no exception. Posidius never seemed in haste to engage. He understood that a key ingredient for this kind of manipulation was an organic feel. His approach was natural. Their conversations began on seemingly inconsequential topics, the kind that filled the halls and gardens of the palace with the mundane chatter of nobility. Yet, with each exchange, there existed a subtlety. With an almost invisible hand, Posidius steered their dialogue with finesse.

Taxation was the first of the weightier subjects to surface, a matter of perennial debate among the court. Posidius mused on the implications of the current policies, not seeking immediate responses but planting seeds of thought. The growth of the merchant nobles provided fertile ground for further discussion. This new class of wealth, risen from the mercantile trade, was reshaping the social landscape of Bacrea. Posidius expressed a calculated curiosity about Paterocles' views on this phenomenon, highlighting the traditional nobles' disdain for those whose prestige was not grounded in martial valour or hereditary lands but in the fluid riches of commerce. These discussions were engaging and achieved the aim of disarming Paterocles. They were mere preludes to the subject that laid at the heart of their meetings: the looming spectre of war with Ellisar. Here, Posidius trod lightly, aware of the passion with which Paterocles held his beliefs. The topic was broached not as a matter of debate but as a concern for the realm's future, a shared worry that invited confidences rather than confrontation.

As Paterocles spoke of his hopes for diplomacy over war, Posidius listened studiously, absorbing knowledge. It was in these moments, as Paterocles articulated his vision for peace and his perceived folly of war, that the foundation of their scheme was laid. Posidius' responses were thoughtful, reinforcing the prince's convictions while subtly affirming his own role as a confidant and advisor.

Through these carefully guided conversations, Posidius could glean not only Paterocles' stance on key issues but also the depth of his commitment to them. These exchanges, while seemingly benign, provided a platform. They gave Posidius the insight to craft a narrative that mirrored Paterocles' known convictions and concerns.

Within the confines of a chamber reserved for guests, Posidius pondered. The room morphed into a melting pot of conspiracy. He approached the task with deliberation, despite the eagerness from Esevia that filtered to him through Tonare. The room, filled with the soft light of early evening, bore silent witness to the devious craftsmanship. He paced about the room. The steps reflected his measured thoughts, as he sieved through this mental liquid – the nuances of his recent conversations with Paterocles became clear. The prince's stance on the looming conflict with Ellisar, his preference for diplomacy over the clamour of war, and the earnestness that coloured his speech – all served as fodder for Posidius' sinister craft.

The parchment laid on the desk, an untouched field soon to have the ink of discord seep into the fabric. Posidius paused, the thudding of his feet coming to a halt. He leaned over the desk, his gaze fixed on the blank expanse. He pondered Paterocles' tonality, the subtle inflections of concern for his people, and his evident passion for diplomacy. These reflections guided Posidius' hand, not merely to imitate but to embody the prince's voice, twisting his sincere desires into a narrative fraught with betrayal.

Taking his reed pen in hand, Posidius began. Each word was carefully chosen, a delicate balance of echoing Paterocles' known beliefs and injecting the bane of treason within them. The letter spoke of a desire for peace and a concern for the future if conflict was to ignite. It mentioned the possibility of ceding land, and King Sharadin's stance against this. Also, it hinted at the notion that King Sharadin's removal maybe be necessary for peace. The fabrication blurred the lines of plausible diplomacy and outright treachery. As the letter took shape, Posidius found himself admiring the artistry of his deception. Almost nodding to himself, he had no ill feelings toward Paterocles. But power belonged to those ruthless enough to take it or protect it. The document was more than a mere message; it was a weapon, finely honed and ready to strike at the heart of the court's loyalty to Paterocles. With the application of the stolen seal, it would have the guise of credibility, just enough to bypass the mind's defences and cause doubt.

Finally, stepping back, Posidius allowed himself a moment of grim satisfaction. The letter, a masterpiece of manipulation, laid before him, ready to be unleashed upon the unsuspecting court.

3

The day was bustling. Tonare strolled through the corridors, his presence a calm epicentre in the storm of activity that surrounded him. The sounds of jabbering filled his ears as he moved. They were loud at first, then became murmurings as he drifted away. Until he passed another cluster of people. The light of early afternoon flooded the grand windows of

Bacrea's palace. Its hallways buzzed with a palpable energy. In the periphery of his vision, a cadre of servants glided towards the Council Chamber, their figures casting long shadows against the floor. Esevia had given the order, and there wasn't a glint of suspicion in anyone. Among the group, Tonare noticed Ophelia, to the innocent eye she was but a cog in the palace's vast machinery. However, Tonare saw the linchpin in a plan poised to shake the very foundations of the Sharad Dynasty.

Tonare's mind dragged the thoughts of the audacious plan with it, like baggage. Yet this rumination wasn't clear on his face. He thought about the plan being in its last few stages and just how real it was all becoming. Posidius had shown the forged letter to him, a creation of words meant to deceive and manipulate. Its authenticity would be aided by the royal seal's endorsement, a mark that could elevate suspicion to conviction. He turned around to eye the Council Chamber's door, just in time to witness Ophelia's discreet departure. Tonare momentarily got caught in the details of their plot, pondering the choice of pen that had brought Posidius' deceptive prose to life. *Reed pen,* Tonare thought. But he couldn't fully work out why that bothered him.

The throne room meeting was scheduled to take place in the next few days. Although they would feel like mere hours to Tonare. It was there that the letter would find its audience, among the gathered nobles and dignitaries. Tonare made his way outside, thinking that if he could escape the walls of the palace – he could escape the walls of his mind. With this effort, he found himself in the palace gardens, where the sun painted everything with a sprightly clarity. As bright as it was, the sun's warmth was exhibiting truancy. The garden was lively, the stone bench he rested upon was plagued with tiny cavities, vesicular. It was a cold, rugged feeling on his backside when he initially sat down. The garden around him bore the marks of the season, with trees standing bare, their branches stark against the sky, and evergreen shrubs bearing the weight of ice on their drooping leaves.

Wrapped in the comfort of his deerskin mantle, the wool tunic beneath adding a layer of resistance to the day's chill, Tonare presented a figure of contemplation amid the garden's natural splendour. His thoughts, however, wandered to the warmer climes of Ahdia, a stark contrast to his current preoccupations. He acknowledged the passing nods of nobles and courtiers, who were unaware of the consideration taking place beneath. Tonare thought that by now, or at least soon, Ophelia would be returning to the Council Chamber. Putting back the seal after she and Esevia had presided over its use. After that, it was just about waiting. Tonare's thoughts drifted to Paterocles, pondering the prince's fate. *That is possible,* he thought, considering the likelihood of Paterocles losing his position as heir yet preserving his life. *Perhaps there will be enough doubt on both sides to avoid drastic action.* The thought of Nulynia's children crossed his mind, their indifference to court politics clear in his imagination. They would not lament their father's loss of favour; their primary concern would be his presence, his role as their father. Yet, this fleeting comfort shattered as Tonare considered the full implications of the letter. Could the red-headed king, a man perhaps just as ruthless as the other Successors, except for Tyvius, truly overlook an accusation as grave as regicide? Reality's bite was sharp. Pulling Tonare back from the depths of his contemplation to the immediate world around him. The garden, once a refuge, now seemed a mere backdrop to the tumultuous thoughts swirling in his mind. As he sat there, his ambivalence subsided and something else came to the forefront. The scratching feeling he couldn't quite decipher – like something else was happening before his very eyes and yet he was blind to it. *Folger is a mere facade. Esevia would have the power*, he thought. *How did she think of implicating Paterocles in treason so quickly, as well as the steps to get to it? Almost as if she –*

"Dear brother!" Nulynia's voice, bright and unmistakable, travelled through the cool air. Her call breaking Tonare's brooding silence, an unexpected sound. She was appearing in the distance, her figure wrapped in layers of goat's skin, a palette of dark and light browns with streaks of white that blended with the winter landscape yet stood out against the bare branches and frostbitten grass. Tonare's heart skipped, his inner sanctum a little shaken. An indescribable feeling of culpability quickly overshadowed the pleasant surprise at the sight of Nulynia, a cherished sibling. Lifting his purposeless stare from the garden's verdancy, Tonare found his sister's figure growing closer, her caramel hair caught in a dance with the wind. She was oblivious to the remorse her presence invoked. A pang of guilt sharpened within his chest as he observed her carefree approach, so at odds with himself. In that moment, he was acutely aware of the facade he must maintain. His gaze, which had roamed aimlessly over the spells of greenery moments before, now focused intently on Nulynia.

As she neared, Tonare managed a smile, an effort to mask the fact that there were fingers poking at his conscience. He almost had to physically tug at the corners of his mouth to smile. He studied her approach, noting the way her garments swayed with her movements, the lightness in her step, and the warmth radiating from her smile.

"What challenges have the gods bestowed upon you?" Nulynia said curiously, her voice gentle. Tonare rose to greet her, conscious of keeping his facial expressions neutral, his smile steady. Yet, underneath the calm exterior, was a bubbling of contrition, caught between the love for his sister and the stratagems against her husband.

"I am not sure what you speak of, dear sister." Tonare gave an answer, after an embrace in which her grip was firmer than his own.

"You looked gone from this world. I thought the gods may have presented you with an impossible choice," some genuine concern in Nulynia's voice.

Her observation coaxed a grin from Tonare, although he was really smiling at the irony she was unaware of. *"Vita plena est difficile electiones,"* (life is full of difficult choices). Tonare said with a mix of resignation and jest in his voice.

Nulynia's expression brightened with a touch of pride, registering the choice of language used and not so much the meaning of the words. "I see you can still use the tongue of Gelarc," she remarked. Her voice carried a warmth that spoke of shared roots. The Egrosians of Ahdia, embracing the New Tongue primarily, had often made Tonare's fluency with Patin a point of intrigue among his peers. She took a seat beside him; a flash of grimace crossed her features as she commented on the coldness of the stone beneath them. Tonare, now accustomed to the iciness of the bench, merely smiled, acknowledging how the environment here contrasted with the relentless warmth of their childhood in Ahdia. "Amazing, is it not? How the winds here grow cold, and the winds of Ahdia are forever warm. We never knew winter's touch in the days of our youth," he mused, a hint of nostalgia in his words.

As they sat overlooking the scenery that was so different from the landscapes of their childhood, memories of Ahdia flooded back. They reminisced about the days spent under the sun, the laughter that echoed through grand halls, and the adventures under Ahdia's generous skies. It was a moment free of the complexities of their present lives. Tonare, his gaze drifting to the horizon, pondered aloud, "Do you think we would hold them closer to heart if we shared the same mother?" His eyes then fell upon Nulynia's caramel locks, noting the stark contrast to Esevia's fair blonde hair, a visual reminder of the divisions within their family.

Nulynia sighed, her eyes turning thoughtful. "Perhaps it was not our mothers that set us apart, but the circumstances. Father courted a lady-in-waiting and grew to favour her more than mother," she whispered. Her insight cut to the heart of their familial strife, suggesting that it was not blood or lineage that divided them, but the shadows cast by their father Kozin's decisions.

Reflecting on Qivinia, Tonare could understand his father being charmed by her. Qivinia, as bewitching as she was, possessed a certain coldness behind the eyes. This was Tonare's perspective, a trait he also recognised in Esevia and Kozin, the younger. He mused on this, trying to rationalise the emotional distance that seemed to define his relationship with his half-siblings.

As Tonare shared this nostalgic moment with Nulynia, a battle raged within him, a churning sensation in his stomach that grew more intense with every glance at her face. Despite the warmth of their conversation, each smile and flicker of joy in her eyes was a stark reminder of the impending doom he had orchestrated. He wished, if only for a moment, that he was alone, spared the torment of witnessing her happiness, knowing all too well the shadow that loomed over it. The churning feeling morphed into a subtle nausea, a physical manifestation of his guilt. It was one thing to rationalise his actions in the solitude of his own mind, to accept the collateral damage as a necessity in his quest for his birthright. Yet, facing Nulynia, seeing the light in her eyes and the ease of her smile, made the reality of his betrayal palpably real. Now and then, as he forced himself to return her smile, the severity of what was to come pressed heavily upon him.

Tonare's gaze lingered on the brightness of her face, her caramel locks that shimmered in the contrasting light of their surroundings, so different from the world they once knew together. In these moments of closeness, the distance his choices had created between them felt insurmountable. The knowledge that soon she might be without a husband, her children without a father, because of his ploys, was a burden he was prepared to bear, but not one he was ready to face in the light of her present joy.

This internal struggle, the oscillation between a brother's affection and a conspirator's resolve, painted a complex portrait of Tonare. Even as he cherished the present, the spectre of the future – a future he had set in motion – cast a long shadow over their reunion, leaving him to navigate the turbulent waters of guilt and ambition alone.

4

The Gynaeceum thrummed with the warmth of camaraderie and the soft clack of weaving looms. Here, amid the opulent decor and the feminine scents of rose and jasmine, the women of nobility gathered, their fingers deftly weaving threads as they exchanged stories and laughter. Brief moments of gossip, too. Queen Esevia, her hands moving gracefully over her own loom, was the picture of serene authority among them, her presence commanding but not imposing. In the late afternoon, the sun was colliding with the horizon, the light of it slowly eroding away. The air was growing brisk with the promise of an evening chill.

The conversation flowed like a stream in a valley, from trivial palace gossip to matters of greater consequence. It was in one such moment of light-hearted banter that the topic turned to the looming spectre of war and the palpable tension between Paterocles and King Sharadin. Esevia, with skilful manoeuvring, steered the conversation with innocent intrigue, remarking on the frequent discussions between Posidius and Paterocles. "It is possible," she mused aloud, "That Posidius' counsel might bridge the gap between father and son. Allowing them to find common ground." Her words were carefully chosen, designed to linger in the mind. Her eyes sparkled with unspoken knowledge.

As the group delved back into less abrasive subjects, laughter returned, along with the enjoyment of delicacies. Esevia's mind wandered to the matter of Tanitos, however. An obstacle with the potential to rain down on the flames of her plans. Esevia's mind was now disturbed by this notion, although the outward merriment remained. She had an idea of how to remove him from the equation, but the scheme wasn't fully thought-out. She had the key ingredients though... The queen excused herself with a promise to return. Her servants, ever attentive, draped her in winter garments, including a bear skin shawl that enveloped her shoulders, transforming her into an image of regal fortitude against the cold.

Stepping out from the warmth of the Gynaeceum, Esevia's face and demeanour conveyed a conventional courtesy. The coldness of the outside world was strikingly different to the room she had left behind, yet it mirrored the focused chill of her intentions. Hidden beneath the surface of politeness, her mind raced with plans.

The queen's steps led her towards the medicus' quarters, a trip made under the appearance of a casual visit, but the true intent was as sharp as a blade's edge. Esevia contemplated her need for Sweet Lily from the medicus. The herb represented the last piece to stitch together her scheme. She expected questions, his need to understand the circumstances before prescribing. Her mind, ever strategising, started to consider plausibilities. Twirling in her mental cylinder, she thought of using her servants' health as a pretext for the acquisition.

On arrival, Esevia's entrance into the medicus' chamber was as deliberate as it was authoritative. She pushed the door open without the courtesy of a knock, her presence immediately causing disruption. The room, heavy with the scents of herbs and chemical compounds, was a visual testament to a man's dedication to medicine. The medicus, deeply engrossed in his work, did not immediately notice the royal intrusion. It was the quietude of the room that was initially disturbed. The queen laid eyes upon a man perched amid shelves overcrowded with medical paraphernalia, the room tight. His hands moved with practiced precision, mixing and grinding, lost in his own world. Esevia, so accustomed to instant recognition, stood rapidly losing tolerance. With an obvious note of impatience, she emitted a sharp "Ahem." He paused. The sudden sound was a sword slicing through the silence, forcing him to acknowledge her presence. It was amazing how quickly the fever of apology took him. He straightened, a quick bow accompanying "Autokratia," a term that underscored her authority. He followed up with, "Grant me pardons." Then, a stillness fell over the room as the medicus' gaze settled on the queen's face. Eyebrows, well defined and arched, accentuated her eyes. Prominent cheek bones, a gently tapered jawline and a narrow bridge nose formed Esevia's face. All of this sat behind the penetrating stare of the queen.

"What brings you to my chambers, Autokratia?" he enquired, regaining his composure and searching for words to break the silence.

Esevia stood, eyeing the clutter of his life's work. The earthy smell of aged parchments, piles of it, was now coming to the attention of her nose. She found herself momentarily stalled by the question. Her mind, usually so quick, seemed to scramble in this instance. *What story does this fool need?* she pondered, irritation beginning to nibble. "One of my servants has been experiencing restlessness at night," she said, unconsciously. Assembling the lie as she spoke, as if the act was an instinctive reflex in the face of danger. "It is becoming a hindrance to her duties. I was hoping for some Sweet Lily Root, to bless the poor girl with a visit to the realm of slumber."

The medicus nodded, his professional curiosity piqued. He started thinking about the necessary steps before diagnosis, forgetting the authority behind the request. He turned from her, his frame covered in a loose-fitting tunic made from a sturdy fabric. The medicus was now sifting through parchments and other paraphernalia. He spoke amid his enthusiastic search. "Of course, Autokratia.

However, a full assessment of the girl would be necessary. It is vital to understand the root cause of her ailment to prescribe appropriately." His response, marked by a firm belief in procedure.

Esevia's steps towards the medicus were deliberate, her eyes sweeping over the alcove with an undisguised disdain. The medicus' sanctuary, cluttered with vials, parchments, and countless tokens of his life's work, laid bare under her critical gaze. Despite the disarray, there was a method to the madness, a representation of dedication that even Esevia, with all her scorn, could not help but acknowledge. "Your devotion to your craft is commendable," she began, attempting to placate. She reminded him of the offer from King Sharadin for more comfortable accommodations - an offer he declined in favour of remaining ensconced within the belly of his medicinal world. The medicus, momentarily buoyed by the recognition, faced her. He presented a face etched with wrinkles; grooves carved by years of concentration.

"Yet," Esevia pressed on, the warmth of her tone feigning politeness, "I find your insistence on an assessment to be a tedious formality. I wish not to insult your craft, but the girl simply needs to sleep." Her irritation was growing as she watched him turn back to his cluttered workbench, intent on continuing his search. "The girl needs nothing more than a good sleep," she insisted.

Her facade of concern shattered as the medicus, still rummaging through his shelves, repeated his professional mantra: "Understanding the ailment is crucial, Autokratia. There could be many causes; physical conditions, black bile–"

It was then that Esevia's patience snapped. "He needs to sleep," she blurted out. *He...* The error slipping through the cracks of her lie. "Are you refusing your queen?" she demanded, the full force of her royal stature bearing down upon him.

The medicus halted, but not because of the enforcement of the royal position. It was the discrepancy in her story that caught his attention. "He? I thought the ailment was in a girl. These things make a difference..." He began, only to be cut off as he turned to find Esevia standing ominously close, her presence imposing and seeming to tower due to him sitting. Before he could utter another word, Esevia's hand shot out. There was a frenzy as the sound of rustling fabric filled the air. In her grasp, wool and testes, there was a cruel squeeze. His pained groan filled the room, a stark reminder of the disparity in their power.

"Do not dare to contradict me, you shit," Esevia whispered, only inches away from his face. His hair, a mane of silver, became dishevelled as he thrashed in pain. "I will send you to the underworld, to be fucked in every hole." The blue-greyish eyes peered into the medicus. "You will provide what I require, with no opposition." Her command was not a request but a decree, one that brooked no argument.

Beneath the heaviness of her gaze, the medicus agreed, a mix of fear and resignation marking his features. As Esevia released her grip, stepping back to survey the man she had reduced to a mere instrument of her will, the dynamics of power within the room were unmistakably clear. Esevia, unyielding and formidable, had demonstrated the lengths to which she was willing to go to advance her schemes.

THE CHEERFUL ONES

284 BM

1

Tonare found solace in solitude, yet his mind was anything but peaceful. In the quiet of his chamber, he stood motionless before the large window that framed the relentless grey of the Bacrean Sea. The cold, turbulent waters mirrored his inner world, a prelude to the storm that was about to unfold in the Throne Room. Wrapped in fabrics of deep indigo, his attire exuded a sombre vibe. The colour, normally perceived as rich, appeared muted. The blue was more like twilight shadows than violet blooms in spring. His dark blonde hair, a few inches longer since his arrival in Bacrea, cascaded at the side of his face, a testament to the passage of time in a land that he had fled to in pursuit of his ambitions.

A low, respectful knock broke the trance. "My liege," came Posidius' voice, soft yet carrying an undercurrent of urgency. Tonare, his gaze still fixed on the clamorous sea, voiced permission for Posidius to enter. As the door opened, Tonare didn't turn to offer a greeting; instead, he remained transfixed by the view outside, where thick grey clouds loomed, cold and unyielding, with no chance of sunlight piercing through the dense coverage. Posidius stepped into the room, his eyes immediately focusing on Tonare's figure against the window. Words weren't necessary. He understood the weight on Tonare's mind, the prince's burden made visible by his rigid stance and distant gaze. Beyond Tonare, Posidius noted the relentless grey of the sky. The images allowed him to feel the coldness of the outside.

Posidius took a seat, permitting the prince to indulge in his trance a few moments longer before he drew his attention to the Throne Room meeting. Tonare, without request, began recounting his visit to Ophelia's chamber the previous day. Interestingly, he spoke as if talking to himself aloud, rather than communicating with Posidius. Ophelia had divulged Esevia's intentions to use Sweet Lily Root on Tanitos, a plan as dangerous as it was desperate. This was Posidius' opinion. "We must hope the queen is well-acquainted with the correct dosage," Posidius remarked after hearing of the plot, his voice laced with concern. Sweet Lily Root was notoriously potent, and even the smallest miscalculation could have dire consequences.

While on the topic of misjudgement, Posidius shared his concern towards the prince's personal commitments. Aware of the agreement Tonare had struck with Ophelia, he felt compelled to question whether the prince truly intended to honour his promise of marriage. "Are you truly prepared to fulfil that vow?" he asked cautiously. Tonare's response, veiled in ambiguity, was delivered with a tone so devoid of sincerity.

The conversation took an unexpected swing as Tonare's thoughts drifted to the festival of Otia, currently being celebrated in Ahdia. Known to the Egrosians as 'The Cheerful Ones,' the festival's name carried a cruel irony for Tonare, who found little reason for joy amidst the bubbling conspiracy. Posidius, momentarily caught off guard by the sudden shift, acknowledged the festival's significance. He knew of Tonare's fondness for the celebration. With all the scheming, he had almost forgotten the prince's deep respect for the goddess, which he reserved exclusively for her when addressed by her true name - Otia.

"Are you aware of the festival's name in the New Tongue?" Tonare asked, his voice sombre.

"The Cheerful Ones," Posidius replied. Then, slowly, the depth of Tonare's irony became clear to him. The stark contrast between the festival's joyous intent and their current grim reality.

"Not much to be cheerful about today," Tonare murmured, his gaze finally breaking from the sea to meet Posidius' understanding eyes.

2

Esevia's arrival at Tanitos' door was both expected and dreaded. Her knock was soft and carried the doom of the impending intrigue. The sound resonated through the silent corridor, like a prelude to a swan song.

"Tanitos," she called, her voice usually unequivocally commanding, shook a little with apprehension. She entered without waiting, a deliberate assertion of her status and intent. The chamber revealed Tanitos in an unexpectedly vulnerable state, his night garments revealed more than they hid, a contrast to his usual composed and dignified appearance in the court. In the face of the overcast sky, the chamber was awash with a soft light, thanks to the large window with its drapes elegantly parted. This room, his sanctuary, was a place of order and calm, with every item meticulously placed.

As Tanitos greeted her, his voice hinted at the unease within. Esevia paused to take in the chamber. It spoke volumes of the man's discipline. The cold hearth, the neatly arranged furniture, and the stone floor so clean it could have mirrored the sky. It was a discipline born not from an imposed regime, but a profound respect for organisation.

"I thought we might share a cup of wine. I have already tasked a servant with fetching it," Esevia stated, her gaze finally resting on Tanitos. "The winter assembly encourages my nerves." The pretext was thin, and she knew it. To the primarch, it was almost translucent. Yet, he humoured her. Tanitos stood by his bed, subtly twiddling his garments. He politely and cautiously enquired about her nervousness, asking why she didn't seem to display this anxiety in the face of war. This was a jab at her 'share a cup of wine' facade. "One can control their actions better than they can control winter. With the right actions, war can be won," Esevia's response was sharp and confident. Tanitos took a glimpse through the window and saw thick grey clouds that hung oppressively low over the Bacrean Sea. *Yes, I see,* he murmured to himself, before looking at the queen curiously – he saw traits he recognised as both admirable and dangerous.

The wine entered the room, carried in by a servant man whose chiton had faded to a soft echo of its former vibrancy, yet remained clean. He moved with briskness. Nothing about his manner indicated a novitiate. With a quiet reverence, he placed the wooden tray, bearing a small jug and two cups, on the little table between them and departed with the same swift silence, leaving behind a tension that would only grow.

Tanitos' gaze lingered on the tray. He struggled to hide the dismay that took his face. "I must be honest, Autokratia," he began. His voice sounded weary as he moved. A subtle grimace of pain briefly crossing his features as he relied on his good leg. Each step was measured to cope with the pain. His old baggy eyes winced a little as he quickly regarded Esevia. "My tolerance," he continued, pausing to steady himself with a hand against the back of a chair, "Is not what it once was." He limped over to the larnax terracotta, his movements deliberate, as if each step was a carefully considered decision. "For this reason," he added, reaching the larnax and gently lifting its lid to reveal the neatly arranged garments inside, "It is unwise for me to partake before the winter assembly." His hands hovered over the fabric, selecting his attire with the precision of a man who understood the importance of appearances, his back to Esevia.

As Tanitos disrobed to change into his formal wear, he could feel Esevia capturing him with her eyes. Each piece of his night garment that fell away seemed to strip him not just of cloth but of dignity. He felt so self-conscious, the youthful days now so far behind him. Tanitos sensed that Esevia's failure to offer courtesy was deliberate, her stare an inconsiderate invasion. Though he craved the privacy that his rank deserved, he refrained from voicing this need. As his bare flesh was exposed, the queen looked on with a cold disinterest that seemed to measure his every flaw. The aging primarch's body, far from the firmness of youth, was now marked by the signs of time: kyphosis arched his back, and his once taut skin sagged, particularly around the buttocks.

Finally, having seen enough, Esevia turned away, dismissing the sight of his frailty as she returned to the matter of wine. "I know you to be a man of proper manners. Will you really refuse the Pareenum?" she asked, her voice cloaked in politeness but edged with a sharp challenge.

Tanitos shifted slightly, turning to the side, allowing him a cautious glance at her. He carefully chose his words, a subtle firmness in his voice. "With respect Autokratia," he replied, his gaze meeting hers only fleetingly, "That right is only afforded to the Autokrator."

The primarch turned his back to resume dressing. He edged closer to the larnax, each step careful to minimise pressure on his bad leg. His limp was pronounced, an enduring discomfort. With Tanitos' back to her, Esevia made no attempt to contain the annoyance that possessed her face. Tanitos had correctly pointed out that the privilege of not having wine refused, when offered, traditionally applied only to the king. It wasn't a right the queen could claim, yet here she was, attempting to use this cultural norm as a facade to ensure he drank from the cup she so urgently needed him to.

Esevia's hand slipped into the folds of her garment, fingers pinching the small vial hidden there. This was the chance, yet in the presence of this opportunity, a wave of anxiety washed over her. She hadn't consulted the medicus about the proper dosage. That didn't cross her mind when she forcefully retrieved the medicine from the royal apothecary. Her mind churned like a maelstrom, swirling between calculations and fears.

He could turn at any moment, and she had to decide. Too little of the substance, and Tanitos would merely suffer a mild drowsiness, easily conquered by a breath of fresh air. Too much, however, and the consequences could be dire, possibly even fatal. Which error would she prefer to make? Time was running out. Panic seized her. In a rash decision, Esevia uncorked the vial and emptied its entire contents into the cup of wine. As the last drops fell, she quickly tucked the empty vial away, her heart pounding in her chest.

Tanitos, now fully dressed in his gleamingly white himation, turned to face Esevia. His attire, immaculately white and draped elegantly over his frame. As he turned, Esevia adjusted her expression to one of composure, her gaze emitting authority.

Esevia's eyes, often likened to the ever-changing hues of the Bacrean Sea, didn't display their characteristic vibrant blue today. Instead, they mirrored the overcast skies outside – cold, steely grey, and unnervingly detached. Tanitos slowly took his seat across from her, the weight of her stare pressing down on the room like the heavy clouds above. He hesitated for a moment, contemplating whether to remind her that the Pareenum – a social norm involving the king offering wine – didn't apply to their situation, but her intense gaze stole the life from any words before they could form.

"I have always admired the focus in your eyes when you squint," Esevia remarked casually. Her eyes scanned the room, noting its tidiness. "How well kept your surroundings are."

"You are a woman that commands much admiration yourself, to be considered a goddess in-"

"A goddess you intend to not drink with," Esevia cut him off sharply. "I come to you expressing my nerves, and you refuse me." She took a deliberate sip from her cup, her eyes never leaving his. "Insult I taste."

Tanitos recognised the emotional manipulation in her words, yet it wasn't the sharpness of her rebuke that swayed him. There was something eerily compelling about her stare that held him – a silence commanding his compliance. As if moved by an unseen force, he reached for his own cup, his movements slow and somewhat reluctant.

"May Byra bless us this winter," Esevia said, her voice smooth as she smiled. She watched him bring the cup to his lips, studying him.

Tanitos winced slightly as the liquid touched his tongue, the unexpected sourness causing him to pause. "This... Sour taste is unlike the wine of our lands," he muttered, setting the cup down with a grimace.

Esevia's heart sank. She hadn't anticipated that the entire Sweet Lily Root vial would alter the wine's flavour so distinctly. As panic flickered across her features, she quickly masked it with a composed smile. "It is probably a bad batch," she apologised with feigned concern, hoping the initial gulp he had taken would suffice.

Tanitos wondered, if that's true, why didn't they share the same reaction?

3

There was a deep groan of metal on metal. The twenty feet tall bronze doors, darkened to near blackness, swung open. As they revealed the heart of Bacrean sovereignty, a place where power was felt as much as seen, they seemed to part the very air. Suspended between the marble pillars, regal banners of red silk billowed softly, their gold-hemmed edges catching the occasional draft that meandered through the room. Upon each banner, the embroidered visages of deities – Byra, Sanoma, Yius, and Thaton – stood as silent sentinels. They watched over the court, the subtle movement of the fabric making them seem almost alive.

The nave, a broad expanse just within the reach of the heavy doors' echo, became a gathering place of whispers. Here, the dignitaries from Egros' distant reaches and Throcos' olive-laden fields melded with Bacrea's local aristocracy. Each was a portrait of restrained opulence, their brocades a symphony of hues – clung to them with a certain refinement. None dared to don the royal red in a quiet ode to the family upon the throne. Eyes flickered upwards to scan the pillars from base to crown, examining grapevine motifs that encircled.

The murmur of discussions rose and fell among the assembly, complimented by the sporadic flapping of silk banners. Beneath the stoic gaze of the gods, the nobles navigated a sea of political discourse filled with the tribulations of winter, the strategies for war, and the vital matter of grain. Such conversations were paused when a procession of red sauntered through the bronze doors. A sombre colour entered through the Throne Room's perforations, causing a slight dimming of the brilliance within. They entered, drawing the eyes of the assembled nobles, noticeably incomplete without the king amongst their number.

Esevia moved gracefully through the assembly, flanked by her children and those of the king's first marriage. An obvious line distinguished her own progeny from her stepchildren. Their tunics and peploi were bright, yet it was the queen's presence that especially commanded the room's attention. After a brief glance at Paterocles and Nulynia, Esevia turned her full attention to the nobles who greeted her, their heads bowed, offering their respect with a reverent "Autokratia," their compliments flowing freely. The stark red of her attire intensified the pallor of her skin, the vibrant hue a sharp contrast that seemed to draw all eyes to her. Her lips were tinted deep red with the stain of alkanet root.

Pleasantries were exchanged, with idle speculation threading through their conversations. Esevia's mind intermittently dashed to Tanitos; the plot rested like a coiled serpent on her chest. In the moments of these fleeting lapses, a fine unease washed over her features. It likely went unnoticed, both by her and the throng of onlookers. But a noble from Throcos, dressed more ostentatiously than his peers, noted the brief moments of Esevia's disquietude.

"Autokratia," he began with a flourish befitting his appearance, the gold on his hands clinking softly. "Is there a cause for concern?"

Esevia's blue-greyish eyes snapped back to the room, the unease expelled as quickly as it had appeared. She offered the nobleman the smile that formed. "It is nothing, no cause for concern," she assured. The placidity fully restored, and her voice sounded well-rehearsed, a composure as smooth as the marbled floors beneath their feet.

Amongst a sea of nobility, Ophelia stood on the periphery in the company of the other humble servants. Her heart pounded beneath her unassuming exterior, fingers trembling slightly as she clutched the folds of her chiton. It had a rough and robust feel. The Throne Room swelled with the pomp of the assembly, nobles streaming in like a tide of opulence and power. Against the backdrop of the red banners, their robes swirled, a kaleidoscope of colours. Ophelia caught glimpses of gold and silver threads in a muted glow, gemstones that were attractive even though they didn't sparkle. She marvelled, not with a yearning for their status or material possessions, but with a pang for the autonomy they wielded – freedom to speak, to choose, to live, which seemed as distant to her as the Far East.

Servants were mere shadows, seen but not heard, or in Ophelia's case, neither seen nor heard. Yet, they had a role to play, carrying trays of wine and delicacies around the assembly at intervals, their presence a discreet dance of service and silence. She tried her best to shrink her presence, but the conspiracy she was a part of made her feel so conspicuous. She could hear the thud of her heartbeat.

As Ophelia brushed against luxurious materials, a sudden recollection gripped her - the sensation of the parchment against her skin as she placed the forgery amongst the other missives. The memory, so intense that for a moment, she was transported back to that instant. Her breath caught in her throat.

She shook her head almost imperceptibly, attempting to dispel the anxiety that clung to her like the early morning mist on verdant hills. Ophelia's gaze landed on Escvia, the queen's imposing presence looming over the room. Her task now completed, Ophelia retreated to the edge of the room once more, her eyes skimming the crowd, always observing, always waiting. A knot of apprehension coiled tighter within her, but it was not just for the forgery or the chaos it might unleash. No, her anxiousness stemmed from something else, a secret that would be revealed in the coming moments.

4

Tonare and Posidius entered. Their deep indigo garments, a bold contrast to the surrounding extravagance. Standing at the opening, flanked by towering doors, they observed a sea of flashy colours and frivolous laughter. Upon their faces, an imperturbable expression rest, a necessary mask for the formalities. Before they stepped further into the opulent party, Posidius turned to his prince, his voice low and serious. "My liege, what is it that drives your ambitions?"

Tonare met his loyal advisor's gaze with an intensity. Posidius couldn't decipher if it was determination or obsession shining in those eyes. "Imagine having your life shaped on the idea you were destined for something. Only to have that thing removed from your grasp," Tonare replied, his voice bitter. Posidius had barely begun to process this revelation when Tonare turned the tables and asked his own question. "And what drives you to stand by me, even on this treacherous path?"

There was no immediate response. Then the quiet stretched on, swelling into an uneasy hush that seemed to fill the space between them. Tonare shifted slightly, his own question hanging in the air, unanswered. Had Posidius not heard him, or was there another reason for the delay? As the silence took on a presence of its own, Tonare's curiosity deepened. He was unaware that Posidius wrestled with a truth – a revelation that the prince did not share. On the cusp of prompting Posidius once more, Tonare caught a subtle change in his advisor's demeanour, a readiness to speak that hadn't been there moments before.

"Excelletem," Posidius finally replied. "Just as you have taken a vow of death in your promise to Ophelia. So too have I sworn an oath. Your cause is my cause, your fate is my fate."

Tonare's eyes widened in surprise, not knowing that Posidius had also sworn a vow of death. But the implementation of such wasn't a surprise when he considered his father's character. After losing favour in the line of succession, Posidius' unwavering support was a source of comfort, something his father gave him that didn't now feel empty. The golden sceptre he owned seemed like a theatrical prop, a reminder of the imperial authority he was denied. Tonare and Posidius moved into the assembly. The lively buzz of conversation enveloped them. The nobles, their laughter echoing under the high barrel vaults of the Throne Room, immediately greeted them. "Ah, here are men that know only the relentless heat of Ahdia?" joked a noble from Egros, his eyes twinkling with mirth. "Will you survive winter's chill, or shall we expect you to turn to ice?" he continued, the humour lightening the political tensions.

Tonare managed a tight smile, his gaze momentarily drifting to the periphery of the gathering. There, subtly blending with the other servants, he spotted Ophelia. Her face conveyed a heaviness that seemed to weigh down her entire being. When their eyes met, she quickly averted her gaze. Her delicate features were contorted with a mix of emotions Tonare couldn't quite decipher, leaving him with an unsettling feeling – an odd vibe. He was just about to delve deeper into his thoughts – when a flamboyant noble from Throcos approached, snapping his attention back to the conversation.

The Throcos, noble, clad in a loudly decorated robe that boasted the lush greens of his region, broke away from the cluster around Esevia and joined them. As he approached, the gentle rustle of his robe was overshadowed by the distinct clacking of the many bangles encircling his forearms, announcing his arrival. "While we in Throcos may not have the fiery skies of Ahdia or Copia, we take pride in our fertile lands," he said, gesturing animatedly. "Olives especially grow abundantly."

"Indeed, they do," Tonare replied, nodding. "Posidius here is a son of the island, and his family are well-regarded olive merchants." He used the opportunity to segue into a topic less fraught with personal stakes. "But the uniqueness of Ahdia is not found solely in its constant sun. It is the inundation of the river that breathes life into the grains, sustaining the fields that feed the people." As they conversed, Tonare angled himself so that he could monitor Ophelia without making it obvious. From his vantage point, near one of the grand columns with silk banners quietly flapping, he watched her interact with other servants. Her preoccupied mind, discernible even from a distance.

The noble from Throcos nodded appreciatively, clearly intrigued. "Ah, water and sun in harmony," he mused. "During my time trading, I have heard of a structure built by the burnt face ones, said to measure the river's flood and predict the yield of the land. How incredible must a mind be to-"

"It is not something they attribute to acumen, good Addrius," Posidius interrupted.

"Yes, their harmony with the Loom is the explanation they give for such structures... As well as other things," Tonare added.

"Ah, I see," Addrius said, the intrigue visible on his face.

The conversation flowed, but Tonare's mind was elsewhere. Something about Ophelia's image nagged him. He was trying to find the word for the emo–

Paterocles, having left Nulynia surrounded by a circle of inquisitive nobles, edged towards the gathering of aristocrats where Tonare and Posidius stood. The conversation about the burnt face ones was reaching a peak just as he approached. Moving slowly, with an apologetic manner that acknowledged his intrusion, Paterocles' attire – less ostentatious than that of many other nobles but distinguished by a bold colour and high-quality material – made him stand out. The group quickly noticed his presence. He greeted the nobles with a courteous nod. Tonare's train of thought was disturbed. Paterocles then specifically acknowledged Tonare and Posidius with another nod.

"Pardon the intrusion," Paterocles began. "I believe I heard talks of agriculture and advancements."

"Yes," a noble from Acrua said, donned in yellow. "Good Addrius was just marvelling about a structure in Ahdia, said to measure the inundation and forecast the yield. Prince Tonare was informing us."

"Yes, I have heard of such a structure," Paterocles responded, his eyes turning to Tonare and noticing a tight smile on his face. "Ahdia does possess a certain mystique; my father has always said so. There are many structures one could marvel at, the most obvious would be the Kyboi." The group nodded silently in agreement.

"Magnificence carved from dry land," the noble donned in yellow added.

"Interesting how different cultures harness their environment," Paterocles replied. He then paused thoughtfully, seeing this as an opportunity to share his idea for improvements. "I have been contemplating the development of new civic works in Shaara that might use taxation in a way that significantly improves the quality of life for the commoners," Paterocles stated. The unenthusiastic expressions spread across the group like a contagion. Eyes that had once sparkled with intrigue now faded to dullness, and a few of the nobles shifted uncomfortably, their gazes wandering to the floor or far-off walls. The mention of civic works and the welfare of commoners clearly struck a chord of disinterest, possibly because of the lack of profit such ventures promised. Some nobles exchanged quick, almost unnoticeable glances.

Tonare sensed the stiffness that crept into the previously relaxed atmosphere. "Your plans sound commendable, Paterocles. The realm could benefit from such foresight," he remarked, his voice intended to expel the discomfort attempting to settle. However, beneath this outward display, the words lacked the genuine warmth of conviction. Though Tonare spoke of future advancements, a flicker of doubt in his eyes revealed a deeper concern: the uncertainty of whether Paterocles would even live to see his visions come to fruition. Posidius chose this moment to chime in, just as Paterocles was beginning assessing the doubt on Tonare's face.

"It is always wise to consider the welfare of those whose backs the realm is built upon. Your plans sound like a beacon of progress," Posidius said with genuine respect but also as a strategic move to divert Paterocles' attention from Tonare's scepticism. The support from Posidius caused a hint of a smile to form on Paterocles' lips. The reaction of the other nobles hadn't discouraged him; in fact, he had anticipated their reluctance. What truly mattered to him were the thoughts of individuals like Posidius, whose opinion he held in higher regard.

Paterocles cleared his throat, his eyes twinkling. "You should all remember the labour that turns the grapes into the wine that fills your cups," he said with a mischievous tone. The nobles shifted uncomfortably, some smirking while others appeared to flinch in the face of his candidness.

He then turned to Posidius, his demeanour relaxing. "Posidius, I would like for you to see the areas I wish to improve," Paterocles extended. Without hesitation, he then addressed Tonare with a shift to formality. "Tonare, you are of course welcome, if such things interest you," he added, though the lack of warmth made it evident that this was more a gesture of courtesy than a heartfelt invitation.

Posidius nodded affirmatively. Tonare, after a moment's hesitation, agreed as well. As both men accepted, they stole a quick glance at each other, the fleeting exchange hinting at their shared scepticism over the true likelihood of such a day coming to pass.

Addrius saw an opportunity to add levity to the tense atmosphere. "Ah, if only good intentions were as plentiful as olives in Throcos! But if the gods will it, Excelletem, your vision will become flesh," he proclaimed with a dramatic flourish. His jest garnered a few chuckles, though not enough to kill the underlying tension.

Tonare, however, was unmoved by the feeble attempt at humour. His thoughts were smelling death. *The gods do not will it*; he brooded silently. *The only will that matters now is the queen's*. His eyes glimmered toward Paterocles.

The room's attention was diverted to the entrance suddenly. Tonare perceived a sinister chill. The murmur of hushed conversations was snuffed out, plunging the room into a silence that Tonare found unnerving. Every head turned in unison toward the space between the imposing doors. The Ahdian prince knew he was steadily approaching the reality of his decisions.

5

The space of the Throne Room expanded vast and grand as King Sharadin entered, accompanied by the High Priestess walking gracefully alongside him. Advisory men trailed behind in an organised fashion. Sharadin's eyes briefly scanned the gathering crowd but did not single anyone out; his focus was solely on the throne where he would sit. The group moved purposefully down the long nave, a quietude mixed with awe and reverence filling the air. In that moment, time seemed to become glacial as the High Priestess regarded Tonare. For a fleeting second, it was as though Otia herself was reaching out to him.

Sharadin passed between two groups of chairs organised in neat rows that flanked him on both sides near the end of the nave in front of the ruby throne. Ascending the stone stairs of the dais, he settled onto the throne, and everyone instinctively began to find their designated positions. Nobles swiftly emptied their cups, and servants moved from their posts along the walls to retrieve these empty vessels. The group Tonare was a part of gradually dispersed, each member heading to their appointed areas. Tonare made his way down the nave towards the throne. A servant passed by carrying several emptied cups, but one was noticeably half-filled with wine. Fret glinted in Tonare's eyes as he halted the servant, seized the half-filled cup, and chugged the remaining wine in one swift motion. Handing the emptied cup back, he sent the bewildered servant on his way.

"Gather yourself, Excelletem. This is not the time to become undone," urged Posidius quietly. Tonare nodded in response, then gently squeezed Posidius' shoulder.

The seats in the middle of the nave began filling with nobles, a subtle hum of muttering steadily replacing the silence that had accompanied King Sharadin's entrance. Tonare and Posidius found their places among the nobles, amid a swirl of coloured robes. In the very front row, advisors sat in stark contrast, their white tunics forming a sharp line against the melange of colours behind them. King Sharadin, who seemed to scrutinise the front row intently, drew Tonare's attention. It was then that Tonare noticed an empty seat. Tanitos was missing. A cold realisation washed over him – Esevia had been successful in dosing Tanitos. But what now?

Suddenly, Sharadin gestured for one advisor. The chosen advisor, clothed in his white tunic, ascended the dais steps and leaned in to receive hushed words from the king. Tonare watched curiously as the man descended, then exited the Throne Room accompanied by a servant. Instinctively, Tonare felt a knot tighten in his gut; this was certainly about Tanitos.

The assembly in the Throne Room gradually settled down, with each person finding their seat amongst a growing sense of anticipation. Servants, distinguished in simpler attire, stood on the outskirts of the room, ready to attend to any needs the nobles might have. The air was crisp with the smell of winter freshness, untainted by the usual heavy incense or fragrant oils that were often employed to mask the staleness of old stonework. Competing with this brisk aroma were occasional smoky, woody whiffs from the braziers that punctuated the grand hall, adding to the atmosphere a rustic flavour.

Darius, the master of ceremonies, had arrived, and now took his position. His entrance had been an agonising watch; he moved with a slowness that rivalled Tanitos' own gait, yet he didn't need a cane for support. Some nobles had whispered threats of dragging him to his platform due to his frustratingly slow pace. Darius finally positioned himself on a slightly elevated platform, a modest square that was lower than the throne but still set distinctively between the monarch's seat and the first row of the audience. To the left of the throne sat the High

Priestess, resplendent in her ethereal garb, while the royal family, excluding the king, sat as a group to the right.

As the murmurs and whispers dissipated, the earlier advisor re-entered the Throne Room. He strode up the dais with a purposeful march and leaned into whisper to Sharadin. The king's face, typically an impenetrable mask, flashed with a fleeting expression of worry as the advisor stepped down and found his seat in the front row. Sharadin's eyes filled with concern as he gazed around the room, lingering momentarily on each noble before resting on the royal guards positioned around the outskirts. With a determined effort to refocus on present matters, he cleared his throat loudly; the sound echoing through the vast space. Conversations ceased abruptly, even the most engaging whispers cut short as all eyes turned to him. Stroking his thick red beard, hesitation clear in his eyes, the assembly waited in hushed anticipation to hear their king speak.

"It seems the primarch is unable to join us," Sharadin announced, his voice resonating through the hall. Instantly, the nobles glanced around and mutter amongst themselves. Before their curiosity could erupt into full-blown chatter, the king continued, "The medicus has been fetched." A palpable wave of concern washed over the crowd, silence gripping the room once more. Sharadin's gaze settled on the High Priestess as he concluded, "We can but seek Byra's grace at this time."

Tonare, surrounded by nobles, observed the proceedings with a calm exterior. He mused over the thought that Esevia's plan was progressing as intended. While the overarching concept might have originated from his own mind, and he, along with his advisor, provided the practical means to execute it, the initial spark for this cunning strategy had sprouted from Esevia's intellect. His eyes sought the cluster of red that marked the royal family positioned next to the throne. Deliberately, his gaze evaded Nulynia's face, instead focusing on Queen Esevia. She maintained an impeccable façade, revealing no cracks in her composure.

6

A young boy, the offspring of a noble family, strode into the Throne Room with lively steps, a stark contrast to the weary and solemn entrance of Darius before him. The satchel carried in his hand, crafted from rugged animal hide, bounced lightly with each enthusiastic stride. The doors closed quietly behind him, sealing off the room from the corridors beyond. From her seat adjacent to the throne, Queen Esevia's lips curved into a smile as she observed the youth's spirited demeanour. His presence brought a breath of fresh air to the sombre room. The boy paused near Darius, ready to hand over the various missives he carried.

Positioned to her left, her eldest son, Folger, maintained a slouched posture, appearing mentally disengaged from the assembly. To her right sat Paterocles, and next to him, Nulynia. Esevia leaned towards Paterocles, her voice a muted whisper, "Do you think Tanitos' absence is a result of Winter's Kiss?"

Before Paterocles could respond, Nulynia tilted forward slightly, eyes narrowing as she cast a glance at Esevia. Paterocles replied softly, "He has seen many years. Let us hope rest is all he needs."

Esevia noted the disdain etched in Nulynia's features and decided to fan the flames. She edged forward, peering around Paterocles' frame until she could see Nulynia more clearly. "Good to see you fulfilling your titular duty, dear sister," Esevia remarked, the mockery evinced by her tone. "With your preference for the greenery of your husband's estate, I am surprised to see you facing the expectations of the palace."

Nulynia, wise to the queen's provocations, delivered a performance of calmness. Any traces of agitation were suppressed from her voice as she responded, "I can fulfil my duties. As can my sons when they succeed the throne."

A forced smile curled at the edges of Esevia's mouth, but her eyes glinted with bitterness.

Paterocles cleared his throat audibly, commanding the attention of both Nulynia and Esevia as the winter assembly was preparing to start. The large, high-ceilinged chamber echoed with the quieting murmur of nobility, while the braziers glowed warmly, their light mingled with the diffuse daylight, casting gentle shadows upon the walls. With a subtle, pointed look, Paterocles widened his eyes at Nulynia – a silent reprimand suggesting that her response to the queen's mockery had been too sharp. At that moment, Nulynia felt a pang of isolation, sensing her husband's lack of support. To her, Queen Esevia's bitterness and envy were as palpable as the chair beneath her frame. Leaning close to Paterocles, she whispered with an aggressive urgency, "You do not see her for what she truly is."

As the assembly was officially set to commence, Darius positioned himself at the podium to read the first missive. The room descended into a silence; the kind thick with anticipation of significant announcements. An uncanny intrigue gripped Paterocles; it was the intensity in Nulynia's tone that caught him. Though aware of her disdain for Esevia, he had always chalked up her discomfort to simple familial discord. She had preferred the estate to the palace, disturbed by what she perceived as Esevia's cruel gaze upon her children. Paterocles, interpreting the queen's fervent advocacy for Folger's succession as maternal protectiveness, now wondered if he had overlooked something more sinister, as he watched Esevia straighten Folger's posture with deliberate, almost possessive movements.

The assembly began with Darius reading out missives from the nobles of Copia, particularly noting concerns from the cities of Tirani and Clomon. These communications highlighted the increasing threat of marauders this winter and pinpointed the eastern front as a probable point of incursion should Ellisar decide to invade. The atmosphere tensed as Copian nobles stood to voice their concerns, their stern expressions and urgent tones adding weight to the discourse. In response, King Sharadin announced a decision to redeploy troops from Gelare, specifically from Acrua, citing its robust military numbers, favourable terrain, and strategic naval access.

Several nobles objected, arguing that the presence of troops bolstered the local economy and deterred minor threats. Emotions flared among the conspirators as these passionate exchanges unfolded. Ophelia, pale and on the verge of nausea each time a new scroll was handed to Darius, struggled to mask her anxiety, drawing concerned glances from nearby royal guards. Her pale face made the freckles across her cheeks stand out more distinctly, each one sharply visible against the paleness of her complexion.

Tonare's suspense mounted with each scroll retrieved from the satchel. Beside him, Posidius harboured an internal prayer for calm, his thoughts intensely focused on hoping Tonare could manage his rising anxiety. Meanwhile, Esevia, still rattled by Nulynia's cutting remark, simmered with nervous excitement, barely containing herself with each unrolling of parchment. She awaited the pivotal moment, eager for her meticulously laid plans to unfold.

The young boy, who would barely come up to Darius' waist even if he weren't standing on a small square podium, handed him a few more missives with focused eagerness. Each scroll the courtier apprentice presented felt like torture for Ophelia, her anxiety amplifying with every document. Tonare's knuckles turned white as he tightly interlocked his fingers, pressing his hands against his lips in silence; he was so quiet and still, one could forget he was there.

As Darius unfurled the next scrolls, they revealed troubling news from Monsker, the mountainous region known for its severe winters and unforgiving terrain. Monsker, with its jagged coastal cliffs in the south and flat, less fertile ground to the north, faced an exceptionally harsh winter this year. The letters stressed the dire concerns over grain supply, as the region anticipated it would need significantly more food to survive the season. With no nobles or dignitaries able to make the trip to Bacrea for the Throne Room meeting, there were no first-hand insights or voices to elaborate on the situation. However, it was clear from the tone of the letters that this winter would be brutal for Monsker. After the reading, King Sharadin gestured toward his gold goblet resting on the throne's side table. A servant swiftly emerged from the periphery, filling it with wine. After a few gulps, Sharadin announced with authority that Egros and Acrua, having experienced bountiful harvests, would send their surplus grain to Monsker to ensure their winter survival. An Egrosian noble, standing in objection, criticised Monsker's agricultural efforts and questioned why Bacrea wasn't providing assistance as well.

Posidius stifled a chuckle, thinking he could predict King Sharadin's response. As a former general of E'del, the king had experience in a realm that covered vast territory. Sharadin, citing proximity and accessibility, explained that grain from Egros and Acrua would arrive more easily and without spoiling due to minimal travel distance. A muffled chuckle escaped Posidius again, prompting an offended glance from the Egrosian noble, who was about to speak when King Sharadin intervened.

"He but laughs at the shitwit your question displayed. Regional support within the realm is integral. Should Copia expect Egros to source iron from a land that does not yield such?" stated Sharadin, his tone brooking no dissent as the room fell into a contemplative silence.

The noble from Egros, realising that he couldn't give an appropriate answer to the king's question, offered a brief, albeit stiff, bow. "Autokrator," he uttered respectfully, yet he could not completely hide the frustration in his voice. As he settled back into his chair, his eyes darted sharply towards Posidius, an ugly look of disapproval. Something Tonare didn't appreciate.

Addrius, sitting to Tonare's left and picking up on this silent feud, leaned subtly towards him, his voice a low mumble meant only for the prince's ears. "Give him no thought, Excelletem. I am sure you are aware of Egros' prestige, being an Egrosian yourself. Now, of course, this prestige is to be respected, but some of their nobility believe themselves to be above order." His words were measured, designed to reassure. Tonare absorbed the advice with a nod.

The annual winter assembly continued with discussions veering towards naval patrols and trade routes. The advisors seated in the front row chimed in enthusiastically, proposing various strategies and improvements. Tonare, however, found his attention dividing itself between Ophelia's delicate image and Esevia's bold visage. Nulynia, who stole his gaze momentarily, offered a smile and nod. Although Tonare returned a smile, it was laden with discomfort, a nuance that didn't go unnoticed by those closer to the prince.

As conversations began to fizzle out, the young courtier handed the withered master of ceremonies another missive. Gradually, silence captured the room as everyone awaited Darius to read. The master of ceremonies, upon handling the parchment, registered that the seal was a royal one, and not one from regional aristocracy. This puzzled him because matters specifically concerning the capital and Bacrea were typically discussed outside the winter assembly. As Darius hesitated, the air grew thick with awkwardness; Tonare found himself adjusting in his seat. Stealing a quick glance at Esevia, he noted she was subtly licking her lips, a sight which unsettled him further.

"Darius, remove tongue from arse," King Sharadin's sharp command broke the silence.

"Y-Yes, certainly Autokrator. But I think there may be some mistake," Darius stammered, his voice thin with uncertainty.

Speculative murmurs surged through the assembly, noble heads swivelling to exchange puzzled looks. Tonare and Posidius exchanged knowing glances, playing along while having an inkling of what had stalled Darius. Ophelia, dwarfed by a nearby royal guard and the grand column she stood next to, watched nervously, wondering if this missive was the one to spark calamity.

King Sharadin, sensing the growing unease, gestured for the scroll. A royal guard nearest to Ophelia stepped forward, retrieving the parchment from Darius and handing it to the king. Sharadin half-chuckled upon seeing the royal seal, thinking it an attempted jest. However, amusement soon fled his features as his forehead scrunched, deep lines etching his brow. He broke the seal with a swift motion and began to unfurl the parchment.

Ophelia's eyes became pinned to the floor, her heart pounding in her chest. Tonare braced himself, while Esevia's sinister smile slowly returned, hinting at the brewing tension that was about to unravel.

The letter written in Patin:

Respects at your door, Autokrator Ellisar

In light of our shared history and the looming spectre of conflict that now shadows the lands between us, I find myself compelled to seek a path that veers away from the devastation of war. It is with a heavy heart that I contemplate the sacrifices required for peace, sacrifices I am prepared to make if it means sparing my people from the consequences of war.

The ceding of lands along our shared border has been considered with great reluctance. Yet, if such an offering might cement the foundations of a lasting peace between us, should I not set aside personal reservations for the greater good? These lands, though significant in symbolising the realm's power, hold no value compared to the lives that might be spared.

However, the authority to enact such significant decisions rests heavily upon the shoulders of the current ruler. My father, King Sharadin, holds these lands with a fierce pride, and his conviction towards retention rather than conciliation presents a formidable barrier. In my quest for peace, should any obstacle, no matter how insurmountable it seems, not be navigated with the utmost care and consideration? If the authority were to shift, if perspectives were to be realigned with the urgent need for peace, could we not forge a new path forward?

I ask you, would you not like a future where our children know not the horrors of war? Is the continuation of current authority conducive to this future, or must we seek change to ensure the survival and flourishing of our realms?

I await your counsel on this matter, hopeful that together, we can outline a course that benefits not only our generation but those yet to come.

From the will of Excelletem, Paterocles

7

King Sharadin took his time to read the letter, his marbles scanning from left to right. His face contorted through a series of emotions – confusion, anger, contemplation – as he tried to digest the implications of the missive. The room, initially marked by an awkward quiet with occasional pockets of murmurs, now fell into an eerie silence. The assembly watched the king intently, sensing the ominous significance of the letter even though they were unaware of its contents. Sharadin finished reading the letter, and tension filled the air. One phrase kept echoing in his mind. *Is the continuation of current authority conducive to this future, or must we seek change...*

Sharadin's head rose from the letter in hesitant increments, each pause more deliberate as he finally looked up. His eyes darting around the room to scan the faces of those assembled. His gaze was sharp and accusatory, as if trying to discern if anyone else was privy to the letter's contents or the intent behind them. This silent scrutiny made everyone uneasy; instinctively, they avoided eye contact, fearing that meeting his gaze might somehow implicate them.

After a moment of silence passed, King Sharadin, still holding the letter, rose from the throne and descended the steps. The room's focus, which had been dispersed in anxious glances, immediately converged around him. Each step he took seemed to amplify the moment, his regal presence now the undeniable centre of attention.

Without a word, he handed the letter to a random advisor sitting in the front row. "Examine," he commanded. The terseness of his instruction conveyed a seriousness that was tangible.

The advisor, visibly startled, clutched the letter and unravelled its contents. One by one, his peers gathered around him, the urgency of their movements reflecting their anxiety. They swarmed the letter, their eyes scanning the delicate parchment with intensity, each advisor hoping to glean some crucial piece of information that might explain the king's ominous mood.

Once most of the advisors finished reading the letter, their sights turned to Paterocles. This shift in attention made the rest of the assembly, including King Sharadin, follow suit. Nulynia grew concerned as Paterocles left his seat, bewildered by the stares directed towards him. He approached the group, and the advisors passed the parchment along until it was in Paterocles' hands. He read the letter, and by the end, he was astounded.

"This is absurd," he stated.

An advisor cautiously replied, "Excelletem, the writing does seem to mirror your mind. We have all heard you speak such words."

Another advisor questioned, "Why would he place such damning evidence in a public forum?"

"Perhaps someone who wishes to remain unnamed is trying to bring treachery to light," suggested another voice from the group. The mention of the word *treachery* drew scornful looks from some of his peers. The mention of the word alerted the nobles and Nulynia.

"I am still your prince, and without condemnation from the Autokrator, you will mind your fucking tongue," Paterocles retorted, an unusually aggressive response that showcased he understood the detriment of such an accusation. Paterocles handed the forgery back to an advisor, his face one of repulsion. "Father," he called, stopping King Sharadin as he was about to ascend the dais.

"Autokrator," Sharadin quickly corrected, spinning himself to face Paterocles. His toga of ox-blood fluttered as he turned, and a growing yellow tint was taking his eyes because of illness.

With the king's attention, Paterocles voiced his denial. "I know nothing of this."

"And yet the letter was closed with the royal seal," King Sharadin said, looking at Paterocles inquisitively. "As the counsel have stated, the words mirror your mind." Paterocles knew he couldn't explain how the letter received the royal stamp but denied the words being his own. He could see that his father didn't fully believe him guilty, but wasn't necessarily convinced of his innocence either.

The advisor, whom Paterocles had returned the letter to, studied it during the back and forth between father and son. His eyes scanned the parchment, analysing every stroke and nuance of the handwriting. After some time, the advisor interrupted them. Having observed the prince's writing before – though royalty usually employed the help of scribes – he drew the king's attention to the fact that the writing didn't mirror Paterocles'. The thickness of the strokes couldn't have come from the quill, but rather, he suspected that the writing was formed with a reed pen.

Reed.

8

Tonare sat ill at ease, shifting in his seat as he struggled to match his advisor's composed performance. Posidius' surprise at the mention of treachery seemed genuine, blending naturally with everyone else's reactions. Tonare, however, couldn't conjure up such a performance even if a blade was pressed against his throat. The reality of the situation sharpened painfully when Paterocles, typically a man of gentle aura, reacted forcefully to the accusation of treachery. Paterocles' short and wavy red hair outlined his face, his decently tall and slender frame highlighted by the ceremonial diadem he wore. Despite his attempts to remain composed, Tonare repeatedly glanced at Nulynia, who seemed on the verge of rising from her seat to come to Paterocles' aid. The more he told himself not to look, the stronger the compulsion became. Meanwhile, Ophelia's face remained pointed at the floor, a posture unique among the servants and one that bothered Tonare.

Addrius touched Tonare on the shoulder and muttered, "It is well known that they do not agree on what path to take regarding Ellisar. But Paterocles committing treason?"

Tonare knew the expected response was to share his view on the matter, but he refrained. He couldn't find any words that wouldn't misrepresent his true thoughts – either sounding too sure of Paterocles' innocence or too willing to entertain the possibility of his guilt. Instead, he refocused his attention on the front of the room just as the advisor holding the letter interrupted the king and his son. The advisor, dressed in white, declared that the handwriting did not mirror Paterocles'. Tonare had anticipated this line of reasoning and sat rigidly, but what followed caught him off guard – the advisor pointed out that the thickness of the writing indicated the use of a reed pen, not a quill.

Reed.

The word sent a spark of panic through Tonare as he and Posidius shared a quick, nervous glance.

Annoyance gnawed at Tonare; he now regretted not considering this detail more carefully. He vividly recalled the moment during their meticulous planning when Posidius mentioned using a reed pen to complete the letter. At the time, it had struck him as significant, but he couldn't fully grasp why it was unsettling. The ultimate goal of their scheme hadn't crumbled, but Tonare realised that he and Posidius were now slightly exposed. He anxiously predicted where the advisor's investigation would lead next.

Sharadin was dismissive of the details. "The writing may not be of his hand because a scribe could have composed it." Descending the steps he had once paused on, his sight shifted between the white of the advisor's clothing and the red of Paterocles' attire as he said, "Reed pen... quill pen... there is no difference." The words, feeling so familiar to the heated exchanges he had in the past with his son, were really beginning to trouble him. That phrase from the forged letter echoed in the king's mind again: *Is the continuation of current authority conducive to this future, or must we seek change...*

Tonare knew what was coming next, as he fought the encroaching anxiety with a clenched fist. The advisor tried to add further words, but the king wouldn't listen.

Paterocles defended, "If I were to commit such an act, why would I seek the aid of a scribe who could easily confess his part?"

The advisor attempted words again, but the king brushed him off in favour of replying to the prince. "I do not pretend to know your mind." The king then began to close the distance between him and

Paterocles, "So you deny any knowledge of this letter, even though it bears the royal seal."

"Yes! I know nothing," Paterocles declared.

The king grew wide-eyed before pointing at the High Priestess who was a silent observer. "You swear it! Before Byra's vessel."

"I do!" Paterocles affirmed.

There was a gap, and the advisor successfully wormed his way in. "Autokrator, if I may." *Sanoma's cock, here it comes,* Tonare thought. He locked eyes with Posidius, who was very aware of his habitual error. The advisor finally got it out, "The reed is not something we use in Bacrea, or other associated lands. We do not form missives in such a way. The region known for this is Ahdia."

Fuck, Tonare thought.

The Ahdian prince felt as though all eyes were on him and Posidius, though in reality, they weren't. The assembly was just beginning to digest the advisor's words. Droplets of sweat gathered at his temple, and he felt a warmth slowly possessing him. It wasn't the temperature of the room causing this; it was the type of heat one got from being the centre of undesired attention. Nulynia delayed the scrutiny that was destined to come Tonare and Posidius' way when she could no longer contain herself and rose from her seat.

"Paterocles would never betray the –" Her words stopped short when Paterocles extended his arm, palm out, causing her steps to cease. It wasn't her place to speak. She didn't return to her seat, as she was far too anxious for that.

King Sharadin refocused the matter to the advisor's point and snatched the letter from him to analyse the thickness of the characters for himself. Initially, only the words registered to him, but now he could see the writing of the characters and he realised the characters might not have been written with a quill. "Prince Tonare!" Sharadin's voice rumbled, although not as strong as it used to be.

Tonare rose from his seat in a blink. "Autokrator," he said aloud, while his inner monologue begged him to stay calm.

"Is the quill used in Ahdia for the realm's administration?" the king asked, even though he already knew the answer.

"No, my father, like E'del before him, has taken on many of the customs of the burnt face ones," Tonare replied. The king's line of questioning was evident in his eyes even from the distance Tonare was standing at. Anticipating the next question, the prince of Ahdia asserted, "Autokrator, I assure you I know nothing of the letter you find in your possession."

Esevia smirked in the distance.

King Sharadin eyed Tonare and Posidius intently, his gaze flicking between them and the parchment. Beneath the silky sheen of pigeon blood rubies that plagued his crown, the autocratic figure was deep in thought. His mind churned over the possibilities and implications. Finally, he turned to Dimitos, the advisor to whom he had first given the letter.

"Dimitos, do you think our guests conspired with Paterocles?" The word *conspired* encouraged Paterocles to defend himself once more, but before he could speak, the gesture of Sharadin's index finger stole his words. The king then eyed Dimitos for a response, his red brows lifting in an expectant arc.

Stammering, Dimitos said, "I-I would not reach that conclusion, Autokrator. I simply point to the letter's appearance."

A subtle sigh of relief left Tonare, though his heart still thumped, and his legs felt somewhat unstable. There was a chance the spotlight might leave them soon. But while trying to keep control of the narrative and deceive, by giving Esevia a false sense of security, it was Tonare who was ultimately overconfident and misjudging. The words that came next sent a tremor through him.

9

Queen Esevia watched the unfolding events before her with evil amusement, occasionally playing with Folger's untidy hair. A couple sips of wine had reduced the vibrancy of her lips. She cleaned her lips with a cloth before retrieving more alkanet paste. The paste was stored in the very tip of an ibex horn. It was polished and adorned with patterns, with a fitted lid attached to a small leather cord. She blotted her lips with a cloth lastly. Esevia always intended to draw the assembly's attention to something in particular, but when the matter of the reed pen was brought up, she was delighted. Posidius' mistake, which had come from a force of habit, made what she intended to do easier. She looked across at Ophelia, whose downcast demeanour slightly irritated the queen. The slave was oozing guilt. Next the queen looked at Tonare standing, him saying he knew nothing of the letter, and she smirked thinking: *you tried to fool me, you cunt.*

Esevia rose from her seat after kissing Folger on the forehead. "If I may," she said, gaining the attention of the room. "I say this without any emotional fog, but perhaps Tonare is not the one we should be looking at."

Tonare was a little suspicious at first; but they were co-conspirators, after all. Perhaps she really was coming to his and Posidius' aid. He didn't have much longer to entertain this notion.

Esevia continued, "His right hand, Posidius, would make more sense." A tremor ran through Tonare, one he had no chance of masking. He nearly stumbled, his leg pushing his chair back, and the sharp noise of the drag filled the room. Addrius gave him worried eyes. Tonare wondered why she was drawing attention to Posidius, knowing he was the one who crafted the letter, and that the suggest–

Bing – and that the suggestion for him to do so was *hers.*

Esevia went further. "We have all seen them mingling in recent times. Posidius offering counsel on various matters, no doubt counsel concerning Ellisar. He is skilled in the art of diplomatic affairs. What Paterocles promised him in return for aid, I do not know."

"You vile –" Nulynia launched at the queen. Just before she could lay hands on her, the royal guards intervened. They restrained her arms, her appearance becoming dishevelled as she thrashed with rage, her cheeks flushed. Paterocles warned them against being too forceful, and they heeded this. Nulynia's necklace survived the man-handling.

"Calm!" Sharadin shouted, calling for order. He then instructed Posidius to come to the front of the assembly. Tonare followed almost instinctively, a simple show of support for the only man he could trust.

As soon as Posidius arrived, standing before the king and the full view of the seated nobles, he offered a defence: "Autokrator, I fear this misunderstanding is growing dangerous. I spoke to your son about a great deal of issues, but the notion we conspired to commit regicide... patricide... With the utmost respect, I think Autokratia's judgement is amiss here."

Tonare found it interesting how Posidius could articulate himself so calmly in this precarious situation. He effectively planted doubt into present minds. The king looked around with conflicted eyes. Tanitos' counsel would have been so helpful right now, but that wasn't possible. He gave all the advisors a look that made them start to mutter among themselves. One advisor presented the idea of acquiring a reed pen, having Posidius write, and then place the writings side by side. The others thought this idea splendid; the nobles mumbled approval, and Dimitos was indifferent. Tonare, hearing this idea, felt uneasy and thought he might experience a bowel movement right where he stood. The king, more perplexed than before, wasn't interested. He turned and approached Paterocles.

The redness of his beard surrounded his lips that were pressed together. He appeared somewhat emotional.

"Swear it," King Sharadin said.

"Father, I have sworn it," Paterocles said. "Before you, before By—"

"No. Swear on your mother's memory that you have not contacted Ellisar."

Paterocles was taken aback by the statement. The dilemma gradually showed its ugly face.

Paterocles faced an agonising predicament. Admitting his contact with Ellisar could validate the forgery and brand him a traitor, while lying might destroy his credibility if uncovered. Choosing honesty as a diplomatic strategy risked backfiring due to the inherent secrecy of his contact, potentially heightening suspicions. Conversely, lying to protect himself could prove disastrous if the truth emerged, confirming his treachery. The added moral burden of swearing on his mother's memory intensified the pressure, forcing him to balance integrity, family honour, and the potential fallout of his decision.

Silence thickened the air as Paterocles deliberated; the room's tension was something one could reach out and hold. His mind raced with the implications – should he confess the truth, risking his reputation and possibly his life, or should he lie, securing his immediate safety but risking future disgrace? His mother's memory loomed large, her integrity plucking at the strings of his heart. The nobles' murmurs became an indistinct hum, drowned by the pounding in his chest. Finally, with a deep breath, he chose the path of honesty and stepped into the abyss.

10

Tonare was grateful that Posidius stood by his side, not just for his calm demeanour but for his ability to sow doubt with his words. Posidius spoke with such measured confidence that even the most daunting accusations seemed far-fetched. Tonare's admiration, however, quickly turned to dread as an advisor suggested verifying the handwriting. Clenching his cheeks to maintain his composure, he feared the worst. The idea of a handwriting test sent shivers down his spine, almost causing him to lose control of his gut.

He thought deeply about the queen's actions. Tonare wondered if Esevia had deliberately shifted blame to Posidius because the reed pen could implicate him and his advisor, potentially unravelling the conspiracy. Was the mentioning of Posidius to protect herself? Was it simply an act of self-preservation? No, he recalled, she suggested Posidius compose the letter, providing a compelling reason for him to be the one to do so. She also suggested the idea of Posidius spending more time with Paterocles, to understand his thoughts on war and his vernacular. Damaging Paterocles' reputation was never a path she entertained. Esevia had mentioned treason immediately upon learning of Paterocles contacting Ellisar. And now Tonare's mental cogs were fully greased and turning, Esevia's shock in the Royal Baths didn't seem genuine. But that would mean –

He was momentarily snatched from his inner workings, the king's demand for Paterocles to swear breaking his concentration. *He has already sworn it,* Tonare thought. Returning to his line of reasoning, if Esevia feigned surprise, then she already knew of Paterocles' covert communications. But how would she –

Ophelia.

Tonare's eyes grew wide, his head spinning toward Ophelia so fast he could have snapped his own neck, the length of his dark blonde hair flashing. Ophelia was in the process of looking up until she met Tonare's eyes fleetingly. The speed at which she broke eye contact confirmed his realisation. Ophelia had informed Esevia about Paterocles first. When the queen had, the note slipped to Tonare about meeting her in the Royal Baths; she was already steps ahead of him. She was probably counting on him to bring up Paterocles' letters to Ellisar. Ophelia didn't buy his promise of freedom; she was loyal to Esevia the entire time. He was never in control.

Never.

Tonare escaped his internal disaster to hear the king asking Paterocles to swear on his mother's memory. He immediately recognised the tough choice Paterocles was faced with and was surprised when the prince uttered a confession. The confession was quickly followed by an attempt to explain his desire for peace. However, the prince, the firstborn, barely got any words of explanation out before a pulse of shock was followed by a commotion. Tonare turned his attention to see the king's hands wrapped around Paterocles' neck.

"Nooooo!" Nulynia shrieked, the piercing sound bouncing off the high vaults of the room, the noise almost having its own life and lingering in the ears of everyone, well after she had shrieked.

King Sharadin's hands, similar to those of a gorilla, thick and robust, squeezed hard around Paterocles' neck. The king's face was a torrent of confusion and rage, his features twisted into an ugly mask of emotion as one singular tear left his eye. Paterocles clutched at the mighty hands, robbing him of air, and threatening to rob him of life. The veins in his head and face became strained, his eyes bulged, verging on freeing themselves from their sockets. His face was growing to a colour that matched the red of his clothing.

"Guards!" the High Priestess stood and commanded with authority. At her call, the guards left the periphery, rushing to the prince's aid. Nulynia wriggled violently but couldn't free herself from the grasp of guards holding her back. They prevented her involvement with firm grips, their expressions unmoved and unyielding as they executed their orders to restrain her.

At least four guards, fitted in iron and leather, grappled with all their might to shift the king's weight. Despite their combined strength, prying King Sharadin's hands from Paterocles' neck proved an arduous task. Sharadin, having appeared fatigued and diminished by illness, now seemed to have conjured strength from the very depths of his being. His grip was as solid as iron, and the veins in his forearms bulged with the intensity of his effort. All the nobles had risen from their seats. They were a collection of statues, the enormity of the moment sapping their ability to move or speak. Their faces frozen in shock and horror. Tonare stood in front of them, watching with a mix of dread and a strange, uncanny fascination as the life drained from Paterocles' eyes. The ultimate goal of the scheme was coming to fruition, and he found the reality far more horrific than he had ever imagined. He could hear Nulynia's relentless screeching, a sound so piercing and frantic that it seemed to embed itself in his very soul. He resisted the urge to look her way, knowing that her anguish was too intense to witness directly.

Finally, with a herculean effort, the guards managed to pry the king's hands from Paterocles' neck. But it was too late. No breath remained in the prince, who collapsed lifelessly to the ground. The room was filled with an eerie silence except for Nulynia's sobbing. Released from the guards' grip, she rushed to her husband's side, cradling his head in her bosom, her tears falling freely as she wept. She rocked back and forth, her sobs echoing through the grand hall, enveloping everyone in the rawness of her grief.

King Sharadin, still shaking from the exertion, turned his wrath towards Tonare and Posidius. "You have conspired with him," Sharadin stated, his voice struggling to rumble in the grand hall. Tonare's lips parted to protest, but his words only served to provoke the flames of the king's rage. "You have conspired!" The king's intense eyes now bore into Posidius. "I will have your writing examined, and if there is the smallest resemblance... you both will be put to death."

A quiver travelled from Tonare's spine down to his boots. The icy wave of fear left him frozen by the king's declaration. Yet, beside him, Posidius, ever the composed advisor, squeezed Tonare's shoulder reassuringly. Even in the presence of nerves, Posidius weighed his options carefully. "There is no need for examination," he stated firmly. Tonare flinched at the boldness of the claim, bewildered by his counsel's line of thought.

Posidius continued, "I alone conspired with Paterocles." Tonare tried to interject, but Posidius raised a hand to stop him. "Excelletem knew nothing of this and would have exposed me the moment he knew." The words settled with heavy consequence, while Tonare could do nothing but watch.

Some mouths were open, no one expecting this turn of events. Sharadin's eyes bounced around the room; he could tell many couldn't believe the act he had just committed. With tears beading his eyelashes, he said, "As king of the realm, blessed to sit upon the throne by Byra's grace. I sentence you to die on the grounds of treachery, for betraying the hospitality afforded to you by the people of Bacrea. May you walk in torment and never know the plains of the afterlife, but rather, know the darkness of the underworld."

The room fell dead quiet after Sharadin spoke, a haunting silence that seemed to be its own entity. He gave a nod to a guard, one who had previously struggled to restrain him. Without hesitation, the guard marched up to Posidius, pushing Tonare out of the way, who was paralysed by disbelief. Posidius closed his eyes, bracing for what he knew was coming. The guard, with a firm grip on his spear, plunged it into Posidius' neck. The first volumes of blood were dark, a blackish red. Instinctively, the advisor reached for his neck, not in a true attempt to save his life, but as a reflex to the searing pain. Slowly, he crumbled to the floor, the blood now leaving his mouth. The redness of the blood became more apparent as it spread across the cold stone floor.

Tonare stood numb, his mind struggling to process the events that had just unfolded. It seemed as though most of the surrounding sounds had died, leaving him in a vacuum of disbelief and shock. Nobles, already standing, were beginning to leave the rows of chairs. They moved closer to better see the body now sprawling across the stone floor. Amidst the chaos and movement, Tonare remained motionless, a statue suspended in time.

Taking advantage of the confusion, Esevia left her designated section and approached Tonare from behind. "You thought you could outwit me, brother," she whispered coldly. Her voice was ice, cutting through the muffled din of the room. Every other noise was drowned, yet Tonare could hear her words with piercing clarity. "Promise my slave freedom and attempt to fuck me in arse." Tonare stood, a slightly trembling mess, listening.

"Now you have lost your right hand," Esevia said with mockery, a small laughter escaping her lips. "How will you fare in the game of politics?" She leaned in closer, her tone taking on a sinister edge. "But you must continue regardless... is that not what father taught us? The importance of moving forward no matter what. He had a phrase for that. Do you remember?"

Tonare stood in a daze, the room and its occupants blurring into the background. Yet, the phrase his sister alluded to echoed in his mind, clear as day.

"The ocean is never still…"

I hope this story has captivated your imagination and taken you on a memorable journey. Your feedback is incredibly valuable and helps other readers discover the story. It also provides me with the encouragement and insights needed to continue writing and improving.

Whether you share a few words or a detailed review, your thoughts and reflections would be greatly appreciated. Thank you for being part of this journey and for sharing your experience.

Milton Keynes UK
Ingram Content Group UK Ltd.
UKHW030654130824
446895UK00004B/156